Soul Dancer

Soul Dancer

Lilliana Rose

Infinity Dreaming
Adelaide, Australia

All rights reserved. © 2015 Lilliana Rose

ebook ISBN 978-0-9872133-7-2

print ISBN 978-0-9872133-8-9

www.lillianarose.com

Published by Infinity Dreaming

www.infinitydreaming.com

Cover by Alora Kate

To my sister Sarah,

for always listening to my stories

and believing in them.

1

The gentle drumming signalled the start of the Harvest
Dance. Zarifah took her position behind the transparent
curtain on the stage. She glanced over to where the dancers
stood waiting for the night to be over. Torin blew her a kiss.
Zarifah winked back. He was the closest friend she had here
at the Wolf House and it was nothing more than friendship.
It couldn't be anything more. Ever. Heat flushed on her
cheeks suggested otherwise.

Zarifah raised her arms above her head and closed her eyes,
visualising the dance she was about to perform. She pushed
aside any feelings Torin unexpectedly evoked.

'Now, the lady you've been waiting for,' said The
Presenter. He stood on the other side of the curtain in his
pinstripe suit and top hat, twirling a shiny black cane. 'A
priestess of the night.'

Whistles filtered through the crowd.

'Will your dreams come true tonight? Will she choose

you?' He bowed. 'Enjoy.' He left the stage and the pounding of the drums loudened.

Zarifah held her pose. Torin's image, black hair and sharp blue eyes faded from her mind as she tuned her mind to the dance she was forced to perform. The transparent curtain glided apart. She began to move with the rhythm of heartbeats from the drums. Her arms drifted downwards like a falling feather and rested near her hips. She extended her leg through a gap in the strips of material that hung from her waist and stepped to the front of the intimate stage. Her hips snapped with the drumbeat. Heat built inside Zarifah as she danced, the skill to take a person's emotions surfaced as she allowed the music to guide her. She pushed away the guilt at betraying her faith with the misuse of her skill. *The Regulators will regret their actions against the Soul Dancers.* She did the Harvest Dance to survive. But she also had another reason, which helped to ease the guilt. *They will wish they never enslaved us.*

The room was full tonight, four to five patrons at each round table scattered between the stage and bar. Small electric lights around the edge of the stage gave a seductive feel to the room. A machine puffed out white smoke adding to her allure.

Patrons cheered and leered. Zarifah stilled her tongue against the insults she longed to whip back. She knew better than to speak her mind when dancing on stage. *I'll not be a slave for much longer.*

Zarifah scanned the patrons for someone suitable. She tried

to smell the emotions worth harvesting, a difficult task in the pungent odours in this cauldron of desperation.

Zarifah's hands flowed around her scantily clad body drawing attention to her assets, slowly and deliberately. For now, she could only smell the rotting scent of fear and the bitterness of anger from the patrons, edged with tobacco smoke. *I want something sweeter.*

She allowed her body to surrender to the beat of the drum. Her dark hair was tied in two bundles above each ear, cascaded down with plaits, delicate silver chains and black plastic threads. Her waist showed the unfinished tattoo of enslavement that forced her to harvest. Below her mark the metal belt, tied low, kept her respectable, if that were at all possible in such an establishment. She'd spent hours outside in the cold scavenging for the metal. Her belly button flashed with a golden light in time with her movements. Unpolished fine silver chains hung from her breasts and rattled with her snake-like rolls, as her body begged the patrons to lose their awareness. Bare legs, skin white and stark, tempted the viewers.

The beat of the drums quickened. She had to source emotions to harvest soon.

Inhaling deeply, she caught the scent of cinnamon; the scent of happiness called her. She stepped off the stage and danced towards the patron. No one dared touch her. A House rule strictly enforced. The patrons watched mesmerised. They didn't know what she took from them. The music and the liquor and the dance were all designed so their emotions could be taken from them, as well as the skill of Zarifah as a soul dancer.

Zarifah found the source of the spicy scent. *A Breather.* They looked humanoid but with flat noses, minimal hair. They ate the air, the invisible molecules sustaining them. But the air here on Earth was polluted and such a species would only come to Earth if completing illegal trade. She inhaled deeply savouring the scent as it filled her lungs. *I'll get three more flowers on my belt.*

A series of snake-like movements from Zarifah began the Harvest Dance. Her body stretched like a rubber band and her stomach muscles undulated like ripples in a pond of clean water. The eyes of the Breather weren't as glazed as those of the other patrons, and she had to be careful. The prey had to be in a state of trance before she could start the extraction.

Gradually she moved closer to the Breather, as if she were testing the temperature of water. Her body could only endure one harvest a night and she had to be sure her attempt would be worthwhile. She noticed the bumps on the Breather's neck and the darker colouring. *A female.* A harvest could be completed on anyone, as long as they had emotions. A female alien here at the Wolf House vibrating with happiness caused a warning shiver to slide down Zarifah's back. *A test? From who?* She pushed the questions away. She'd already decided to harvest happiness no matter what. Zarifah's mouth watered as the cinnamon scent wafted around her.

The spicy smell suddenly faded. *I've gone too fast.* Zarifah slowed the dance. To lose the chance of harvesting happiness would leave her feeling more empty than usual. *I won't fail.*

Zarifah's deep brown eyes locked with the Breather's. Her body moved with deliberate purpose of seduction and the cinnamon scent intensified. The pulses of happiness caused her body to vibrate as if a tuning fork.

The connection between them strengthened. The Breather surrendered; Zarifah began to use her skill to move the happiness from the Breather into the collecting crystals around her neck.

Zarifah brushed against the soft skin of the Breather's arms. The patron let out a sigh, yielding further. She straddled the alien, pressing her thighs tight around her legs. Her movements directed the happiness—an invisible energy to others but to her a soft pink coloured gas-like substance—and it flowed towards the empty crystals. The Breather didn't fight, didn't protest. The one emotion that a patron might notice had gone. Once happiness had been taken, it left a void of emptiness that gripped the mind and screamed out the theft.

Her arms guided the energy towards her chest, with her mind and hands, at the same time still moving and stretching her body against the Breather's coarse clothes, quietly begging for more emotion to be released.

The rhythm of the drums quickened, helping the stolen energy to flow to the crystal. The crystals warmed her skin signalling they were full. Zarifah pressed her mouth on the Breather's lips to sever the connection between them. The smell of cinnamon surged through her body. She danced her lips on the Breather's allowing the happiness to linger. The drums fell silent. All Zarifah could think of was the spicy taste of the Breather. Her soul melded with the Breather's. The Happiness flowed through her taking away the memories of this place.

Her mind snapped back into focus. She pushed the alien soul back into her humanoid body and stopped herself from losing herself with the soul of the Breather.

Zarifah danced gracefully away. She could feel the crystals throbbing with the fresh emotion. *I hope it's pure.* The kiss was always a dangerous time for contamination to occur. Tonight for the first time, she had almost pushed what little part remained of her own soul down into the Breather to be taken away. Then she could be an empty shell to be discarded but free. After all, she had once again broken the sacred teachings she cherished and lived for, all for survival on a planet that was doomed for destruction with half the black market of the Universe here on Earth doing business. Another scar formed on her soul.

2

What's a Breather doing here? Zarifah stumbled away from the stage. But that wasn't really what was bothering her. They were expected to harvest emotions from any person or alien regardless of gender. The same rule applied when they were forced to entertain clients in the private rooms. *Where did such happiness come from?* Her trapped soul inside the teardrop crystal on the chain around her neck begged for the happiness that was held in the adjacent crystal. *I need to pray. The goddess Her will give me strength.*

A rough strong hand gripped her arm. Her toned muscles automatically contracted ready to fight back. She spun around to see a Sentinel.

'You bruise me and I won't be able to dance.' She squirmed under the harsh hold.

'Ha, not what I'm told. Some like 'em bruised. You have something valuable around ya neck,' said the Sentinel. 'The Collector wants it now.' He dragged her back to the boss's office, next to the stage where the dancers of the evening stood in line, shivering in their skimpy costumes, waiting to be seen and hopefully given payment.

The Sentinel pushed past the other dancers, some had started drinking the House liquor and were struggling to stand. A few jeered at Zarifah for jumping the queue. She could be in the room for some time if The Collector wanted more than her harvest.

Zarifah's status was delicate. There were other dancers who wanted her place, even though she'd trained them, even though they were breaking Her's sacred teachings. *But I have a plan.* One that Zarifah made with Her during the meditations where she travelled to the space between the physical and spirit plane, to limbo, the astral plane, the place where she could connect with her beloved goddess. *It's a great plan.* The plan to reincarnate Her; to bring back the leader of the soul dancer faith and rise up against the Regulators. *Soon I will no longer help to feed the Regulators by harvesting emotion for them.* The Regulators had been genetically modified; humans without emotion, they were meant to be the salves but they rose up, dominated, and now ruled. Emotions their food source, the dancers were the only ones with the skill to harvest such energy. *I'll be in charge and I can free the other dancers.*

The Collector of Wolf House, Nigil, held a youthful strength in body and mind despite his older age of fifty. He sat behind his desk tallying the night's harvest, distinguished in his deep blue suit, matching vest and jacket. The wolf motif, the House totem pinned on his jacket, reflected the light reminding Zarifah they held the codes for the running of the House. *I must get the pin.*

The Sentinel stood in front of the closed door blocking the exit.

'The Presenter tells me you have been reaping happiness tonight,' said Nigil. He stood and walked towards Zarifah. A heart shaped crystal containing part of his soul pulsed a lustful red hue.

'Let's see now.' The Collector fingered the teardrop soul crystal, the one that held part of her soul and kept her as a slave, bound to the illegal trade of emotions. Zarifah's heart beat anxiously. He was clean yet repulsive all in the same breath. She had almost died countless times in the beginning when she had tried to free her soul using her skills. Bolts of electricity had sent her body convulsing and while the memories were old, the pain still felt fresh. *I'll find a way to re-join my soul.* Determination rippled through her and cleared her mind. *And the souls of the dancers.*

'Hmmm, delicious.' Nigil groaned as his fingers turned the crystal containing the harvest. 'The scent of cinnamon becomes you.' He breathed deeply around her neck before removing the full collecting crystals and replacing them with empty crystals.

'The job of a priestess is never done,' he said trying to provoke her.

'Never.' She was no priestess here. But she didn't take the bait. She looked square into his grey eyes, quietly standing her ground with him. He knew her well, since she'd been brought here nearly fifteen years ago. It was hard to try and fool him.

'See how much happiness the Alchemists can measure.' Nigil handed the precious rock to the Sentinel who went into the adjoining room where the enslaved scientists tested the harvest.

Nigil continued to smell her neck, tormenting her as they waited.

'I've been told you were rather absorbed by her.'

'I wasn't.' She swallowed hard. *I was just reacting to the happiness.*

Nigil smirked as he circled her, tracing his finger around the base of her neck. Zarifah's skin bumped under his touch and sent waves of ripples down through her body.

'Really?' His voice held a mocking tone.

The Sentinel returned to the room. 'It's pure.'

'So how about I allow you to have three flowers added to that pretty belt on your skin if you stay a little longer, just you and me.' Nigil's hands touched her bare waist.

'No.' Zarifah avoided his stare. It was part of their game. She hated being forced into it but she reminded herself there was a bigger plan. The wolf pin glinted silver in the light as he moved his body closer to hers. *Maybe this time I'll get the pin.*

'Don't play hard to get.' His fingers reached further down below her belt.

I'm going to break his neck if he... She breathed in sharply. She stepped back pushing him away. He was quick. He slapped her hard. Her head snapped to the side, her cheek stung and a metallic taste tainted her mouth. She touched her lip. *It's a game. One day I'll make him regret what he's done.* Zarifah stepped forward and traced her bloody finger over his lip. 'I thought that's what you wanted.' She raised her eyebrow invitingly.

Nigil grabbed her around the waist and pulled her to him harshly. He hardened wanting more. *I might be a slave but I'm not helpless.*

Zarifah kissed him. Hard. *It's just a kiss.* A kiss that was much harder to give to him than the one to the female Breather. And it wouldn't stop at a kiss. *I'll do what's necessary for the sake of Her.* She tried not to think of the kiss she gave him, his tongue twisting around hers, or his hands pinching her breast, or his hardness pressing urgently between her legs. She lowered herself to her knees. *I will get my three flowers.*

3

The buzz of the vibrating needles was music to Zarifah as she lay on her stomach on the table while the Ink Master tattooed the payment into her skin. Two small blue forget-me-nots were forming around her right hip along a trail of wavy green vine. She liked the pain. With each bite the needles took to deliver ink she thanked the goddess Her for still watching over her, despite her betrayal by completing the dance to provide emotions to feed the Regulators.

'You've done well tonight,' said the Ink Master, his head close to her skin to make sure his work was perfect. Zarifah was glad to have a tattooist who cared about his work enough. She'd seen many a blotched tattoo ruin a dancer's allure.

'Did you harvest something grand or just a lot?'

'Happiness,' answered Zarifah, her chin rested on her arms. She held back the other words about how it should've been more; how Nigil *the lying prick* had swindled her payment despite her pleasuring him. But in the underworld no one cared about the treatment of those who were owned. And she hadn't managed to steal the wolf pin.

'Explains the spicy smell on you. Though you're not happy.' He wiped away excess ink and blood from her skin.

'Neither are you.' She wished Torin was here getting barbs tattooed to his waist. *He'd be a good distraction.* A hot lustful heat flushed through her body. She swallowed hard pushing such forbidden thoughts away. *It can't happen.*

'What gave me away?' He fell silent concentrating on the last flower.

Zarifah wished he would hurry up and finish. Zarifah couldn't wait to go back to her room and meditate, to release her soul from its physical form and go to the astral plane, the space between worlds, where she could meet the goddess Her and continue the lessons of the Soul Dancers faith. The previous Soul Dancer had told Zarifah about how to find Her. It had taken nearly a year before Zarifah managed to slip into a deep enough trance to be able to send her awareness to the astral plane. Since the first meeting nearly six months ago, Zarifah met regularly with Her, risking severe punishment just to learn the truth about the Soul Dancer faith. That was if she could get Torin out of her mind. There were a few things that she wanted to do to him that sent the moisture pooling between her thighs thick and sweet. *Not yet. I've got to be strong and carry out the plan first.* But she allowed herself a moment to indulge in the daydream where she was slipping her tongue down his salty muscular chest…

'Hey you did well,' said Hayal.

Zarifah twisted around and saw Hayal leaning in the doorway. The dancer had changed into loose pants and a tight top, all black, and twisted her hair up in an elaborate braid.

'Keep still.' The Ink Master pushed Zarifah back down on the table.

'I've one more spider to add to my web tonight,' she said proudly.

'Let me see the card.' He squinted at the electronic chip. His life would be over if The Collector thought he'd added extra to payments.

'You ladies had a good night then.'

'Oh well, you know how it is.' Hayal rested against the table watching the Ink Master work. 'You win some and you lose some. I haven't had a spider for three months, so it was about time the bastard gave me one.'

'What did you harvest?' Zarifah narrowed her eyes at Hayal. Nigil had been harsh on herself but easy on the younger dancer and it annoyed her.

'Nothing as good as you. Let me smell you.' Hayal breathed deeply. 'I'm jealous.'

'Done my lady, go and enjoy the early morning while ya still young enough.' He began to clean the machine. Despite newer technology The Collector refused to upgrade the old machine to lasers, all part of his efforts to save money. Zarifah thought it was more to do with his sadistic nature.

'I wish to dance with you,' said Zarifah as she rolled off the bed. 'We could harvest some great emotions. I'll speak to The Collector?'

'Zarifah you know I've lost the skill, besides who would put artwork on your beautiful young body? No I won't have some butcher thinking they are an artist try and ink you.' He touched the star crystal around his neck that held part of his soul, marking him a slave like everyone here in this House.

He'd been brought here when only a child. He was more like an older brother to her, one she could trust, as much as one could here in the darkness of harvesting. Because of a lack of training, the skill was fading in the dancers. They weren't trained correctly since the records were destroyed by the faith leaders to stop the Regulators from learning the skill. Part of the skill was also inherited. The leaders, Her and Him, would know the families strong in the skill of harvesting emotions through the dance. Again that information was lost. *Not for much longer.* In the hope of restoring the soul dancer faith Zarifah had only told Torin and Hayal about the meditations where she met Her.

Hayal moved onto the bed facing the ceiling. She had only a few spiders on the web around her waist, unlike the flowering vines that covered most of Zarifah's waistline, a tribute to her skill since she had only been dancing for the last seven years. Now at twenty-two she was the youngest and the most powerful dancer in the House, even in the other Houses if rumours could be believed. A title she'd only had for six months, and one that she hoped to use to change things permanently.

'One beastie. I don't even want to know how you managed to get such a high payment from The Collector.' The buzz of the tattoo machine began again. 'You need to be careful.'

'Yes Hayal. Listen to him.' Zarifah leant down and whispered in her ear so the Sentinel outside by the door wouldn't hear.

'Whatever, guys. I have another spider and that is all that matters,' answered Hayal smugly. 'Dark times call for dark solutions, isn't that what you taught me?'

'Yes but I am the Soul Dancer and even I am fearful,' answered Zarifah.

'He did say that I showed the promise of rising to such a position,' said Hayal. Her hazel eyes glowed with the hunger of survival.

'I couldn't think of anyone better to replace me.' Zarifah stroked the young girl's blonde hair. 'After all I have taught you.' She tugged sharply on Hayal's hair.

'Ow.' Hayal turned to pinch Zarifah, but missed.

'I can paint blobs on you instead of flowers and spiders,' he grumbled.

Zarifah left to go back to her own room. Her skin ached where the ink sat in her skin. She worried for Hayal's safety. She was eighteen and still had the over confidence of youth that caused her to make rash decisions. The fading spicy smell still clouded her mind and she longed for more, to help forget about her life.

Once in her room, she berated herself for her behaviour with Nigil. She knew his games, and how to play them, and that she ran the risk of being sold elsewhere. *Like I have a choice.* But still she couldn't get Torin from her mind and guilt stabbed at her stomach as she carefully removing her costume. *I wish I had gotten the wolf pin.*

Zarifah covered her body with an imitation silk robe coloured with dragons intertwining on a red background, one befitting of a Soul Dancer and something that wouldn't irritate her new tattoos. Each of the dancers could choose the symbol of their payments. Zarifah had chosen the blue-forget-me-nots, the flower of the goddess Her; the flower her father used to give her when he went on trading runs between planets and moons. A sign of Zarifah's humour, for she was far from forgotten here, but forgotten by those she loved.

Her room was small and basic, three by three, a grey white finish with a wall of drawers and cupboards held what little she owned and a single bed nestled in the adjacent wall. No windows and nothing on the walls.

She placed two white burning blocks in a black pot and set them alight. She sprinkled the dried eucalyptus leaves into the fire and breathed deeply. The harsh bitter aroma took hold of her mind as she drifted away from her body. Vulnerable, she risked being thrown out if Nigil entered her room.

The scent of the cinnamon on her skin mingled with the eucalyptus and her soul, the part that hadn't been trapped inside the crystal, moved with ease to the astral plane.

Zarifah stood on a mountain side exposed with only rocks and a few tufts of green plants. 'Forgive me, sister, mother of ages, my beloved mentor.' She knelt; coldness seeped into her etheric form.

'I offer myself to you.' A cold breeze stroked her hair. Zarifah lifted her head to see the transparent form of the goddess. She bowed her head again.

'Daughter, you have my blessings,' spoke Her with a soft commanding voice. 'Stand, I know your woes.

'Zarifah, you have to keep harvesting. It is written in the stars, it is why you still live. You are the only one left to restore our existence.' Her's long blonde hair with curls cascaded below her waist and translucent wings, large and glimmering with colour befitting a goddess. 'People will come to you for healing, for you to take away their hate, fear, guilt and anger. It's the responsibility of the Soul Dancer to draw out these emotions, leaving them with a space they can fill with joy and love. This is what we want to restore. This is your motivation.'

Zarifah bent her head with the enormity of her task. She wanted more from the only mother she had ever known who had always given comfort.

'Tell me more. I need to know more about the skill of the dancing I do.'

'The path is set. You risk too much to seek me.' Her levitated upwards, wings pulsing without effort. 'I will tell you all in good time. You must continue my work so that I can join you on earth once more. You will be able to do that if you become The Collector.'

The words caused Zarifah's core to tremble. 'I can't lead the House.'

'You can. Keep training the other dancers, those who are open and willing. That is your task. And get your belt completed around your waist. You have a lot to do. Stop stalling.' Her's overpowering image began to lose form. 'I'm fading here and if I don't reincarnate soon I'll be lost forever. You must work quicker.'

Zarifah bowed her head. 'I'm doing everything that I can...'

'Not fast enough.' She extended her form to full height; her wings stretched out and moved quickly.

A blast of cool air blew through Zarifah and she shivered with fear. 'I'm sorry.'

'Have faith in me. I will help you when the time is right. I must reincarnate soon.'

'Thank you, Mother.' Zarifah automatically spoke the words as her body tugged her soul to return. The mountains became transparent as the concrete walls of her room grew through the rocks and dirt. Her soul was sucked back through the energy layers to the underground of the Earth, following the path she had travelled many times.

Zarifah collapsed, exhausted where she had been sitting, her mind screaming in confusion at the stinging reprimand from Her. She had always followed the instructions of the goddess. A part of Zarifah couldn't help but think that maybe Her really didn't care about the dancers and just wanted to be connected back to the Earth. Back to the life, back to being more real rather than a fading ghost in the astral plane.

4

'Zarifah!' The pounding on her door continued. 'Zarifah! I know you are in there!'

Untangling her body from the floor where she'd slept, Zarifah moved to open the door. The sounds of the morning activities of dancers getting ready to go outside to scavenge filtered along the corridor.

'You look bad, real bad,' said Torin his ice blue eyes full of genuine concern.

And you look more fuckable than usual this morning. She soaked in his features; dark curly hair that was a little damp and his broad stubbled chin that she wanted to run her hands over. *When did this feel more than friendship?* Her body responded with her breath shortening as she lowered her gaze over his tight t-shirt that showed off his taut muscles, down to his black leather-like pants that left nothing to her imagination. *I have resisted him so far.* But she longed to forget about the rules of dancers not being allowed to sleep with each other and take him between her thighs for a night of hot lustful sex. *No, a night and a day at least.*

'You smell bad too.'

'It was a long night. I saw Her.' Zarifah let her robe gape. He smelt of soap fresh, spiced with testosterone that sent her senses on fire because all she wanted to do was to work him into a leathery sweat with her body. She saw him looking down at her exposed skin, and she moved the material a little to let him see more of her breast, but not too much. *I'm just teasing, nothing more.*

Torin moved, exposing the fluoro light behind him. She shielded her eyes automatically. She was now paying the consequences for a poor choice. Last night was full of poor choices. She glanced at Torin who stood close to her, pulsing with heat that melded with hers and sending a hot flush of desire through her and her abdomen muscles contracting with anticipation. *He's another bad choice, but I would enjoy it too much to care.*

'Here.' Swiftly he pulled her smaller framed body to his and kissed her, using his tongue to deposit something small and rectangular into her mouth. She moved it to the side of her cheek and then quickly played her tongue over his. He groaned slightly. Paused and slid his lips slowly off of hers. 'It's my last,' he said quietly.

She leant forward to reconnect with his lips but he pulled away. A fearful shadow cast over his face. This was dangerous territory. They might be seen, and someone would report them to Nigil for a favour. The risk awakened an excitement within her, but before she could make another pass at him he turned away.

'I will see you in ten, make sure you're ready.' He walked down the corridor. 'We've got some scavenging to do.'

Zarifah closed the door. Her heart pounded with a mix of fear and with lust at what had just happened with Torin. *How am I going to stop myself?* Her breath came short and fast. *I can't. And I don't want to.* She groaned, her thoughts pulling her mind in two directions. *I'll find a way.* Determination coursed through her veins setting her heart beating to a more even rhythm. *If the plan works then we can be together.* She was going to make this plan work. *Torin can be my reward.*

Zarifah changed into black thick tights and jumper for the outside walk as her tongue played with the present. She added a few more layers of rough, worn clothes that would barely protect her against the cold.

Sitting on her bed, an alcove in the wall, she removed the rectangular gift from her mouth to see the colour. Red. Moolen. She smiled and sent a blessing to Torin. She poured some recycled water in a dirty glass and dropped in the tablet, swirling vigorously. She wished she could disappear into another form too. Holding her nose against the smell, she drank the liquid and was indebted to Torin once more. An hour out scavenging could make all the difference to how successful things went for her during the next week, especially if she was one of the first out and found the better items that had been dumped the night before.

Zarifah went to meet Torin at the main entrance of the

House. She ran her tongue over her lips and tasted his saltiness. She fought a spell of dizziness and slowed her pace. The tablet was slow to take hold and boost her energy to go out scavenging.

Out of breath, she arrived just as the doors were opening and the members of the House started to file out for a few hours of freedom. Any longer outside and there may be no hope to warm the body and there was the radiation and also the threat from the katners, a furry scavenger evolved from the wastes of Earth, with teeth big that left a nasty bite, could even kill, despite their small cat-sized bodies.

'Thought I may have had to go out alone,' said Torin. He smiled setting Zarifah's pulse blazing with heat. She walked past him and showed her chip to the Sentinel before bracing herself against the cold.

The beautiful plains of grasses and fertile farming land were long gone and the original Wolf House where Her and Him, the leaders of the Soul Dancer Faith had resided, lay in ruins with piles of metallic rubbish, bricks, and concrete spilled out from fallen buildings. Broken space pods, large useless moulds, radioactive drums of waste some leaking green thick juice, and pulled apart engines littered the area. Most of the good parts had been taken over the years, but this was where the rubbish was dumped and it was worth coming out. Piles of metallic rubbish as far as the eye could see, formed small hills on the landscape, thick with waste and smelling of acidic pollution. But there were hidden gems that she and the other dancers could use. Small chains to decorate costumes, metal for a belt, material to be taken apart and refashioned into a skirt or top, as long as you took the time to search and thought creatively, there were things here to help them survive.

'How did you like my gift?' asked Torin.

'Just what I needed,' she said breathlessly stumbling over the rubble. 'Goddess Her help me.'

He held out his hand and she took it. His skin hot on hers sent her heart dancing to an erratic beat. She righted her balance then let go of his hand. *Be careful.* She didn't want Nigil to hurt Torin, which he would if he thought there was something going on between them.

They scrambled deeper into the piles of rubbish. The cold air slapped her exposed cheeks and the warmth from Torin's herculean body reminded her that she was living and that she was hot blooded and ready for him. *Settle down.*

'Looks like there was a delivery or two last night.' Torin pushed open a small pod craft that looked beyond repair. The Regulators, the emotionless people who enslaved the dancers, dumped their waste every few days providing new items to be sorted through.

'You won't find anything in there.' Zarifah picked up bits of metal from the ground. 'Others have been here already.' Members of the Wolf House were hastily rummaging through the piles of scrap ahead of them. Zarifah was annoyed with herself for being too slow and not arriving first. Her chance of finding anything today would be slim and she wanted to make a new costume and then there were always repairs.

'You just have to know what to look for.' Torin's grunted

words disrupted her thoughts. He tried to pull electronics and metal sections apart.

The competition between the members of the House was fierce when scavenging because they also had to fight for the scapes with members from the other Houses. The other Houses had fallen before the Wolf House; Angels, Dragons, Serpents, Condors, and Elephants. The dancers captured and forced into slavery. Sentinels from each House kept an eye on the members to prevent them socialising between Houses. For those who showed cunning there was a chance of trade. The Serpent and Dragon Houses were the worst; they would fight you for something if they wanted it, to the death if they needed to. Angels were ruthless and Zarifah kept away from them. Their bodies had been mutilated and scars formed part of their show. It sickened her to know dancers of the faith were treated like this. *Things will change soon.* She remembered Her's reminder last night. *I'll get that pin. I will find a way.* But there was one thing she was sure of. Better the devil you know, and she was glad that she was in the Wolf House. Nigil didn't treat them as badly as the other Collectors obviously treated their dancers. Nigil was different. An intelligence that he used to manipulate his dancers into thinking that they were being looked after so they would perform better. *Maybe that's why we are the best House, the one that brings in the highest yielding emotions?* At twenty-two, Zarifah was the eldest dancer along with Torin. The Serpent dancers were older, in their thirties. There weren't many dancers after that age. They became Ink Masters, Collectors if they were lucky, maybe Sentinels or Presenters or they were forced to work in the House washing and cleaning until they died.

Zarifah wanted to find small chains since they were the easiest thing out here to use as part of her dancing attire. If not, then she would have to take bits of metal and try to make the chains herself, a time consuming and labour-intensive task for little reward. But like everyone in the House, costumes had to be appealing to ensure a successful harvest.

'You want this bit of plastic tubing from the electronics?' Torin held up a handful of colourful wires.

'Yeah.' She was grateful but dreaded the hours ahead to try and fashion them into something usable. She pushed the handful of small tubes under her jacket. The ends of her fingers were freezing and she decided to keep an eye out for material, as well as metal. Sometimes you could be lucky.

Torin jumped from the pod and went to another nearby pod. Zarifah stumbled through the crap that had been discarded from the races of the Universe. She sent her love to Her and the Earth, despite her mixed feelings towards the goddess after last night. *I can trust Her.* There were twisted metal pipes, sawn off electronics, general garbage leaking toxic chemicals, mixed in a graveyard of rusting and polluting technology. The acidic fumes, putrid and thick caused her to breathe through her mouth. She concentrated searching through the materials. There were plenty of sharp objects, and rusty metal that could cut her if she wasn't careful. They only cuts on her body allowed were to be the ones from clients. And the lack of care Nigil had towards medicine in the House meant that a cut could be dangerous to her life if a bacterial infection took hold.

A horn sounded. The time outside was over. Zarifah collected a few smaller pieces of malleable metal as she climbed down from the pile of scrap.

'Whatcha get, Zarifah?' asked Hayal. Despite being rugged up with a scarf and beanie, the skin around her waist wasn't covered and revealed the spider tattoos.

'You should take more care covering up out here.' Zarifah couldn't help caring for her dancers. 'Bits of plastic and basic metal, nothing much today. You?'

'Well, few chains, some cloth from the new pods.'

'Cloth? You were lucky.'

'Yeah only if I can wash out the blood and alien goo.'

'Get a move on,' yelled a Sentinel. He belted his baton on the gate.

'Bastard,' muttered Hayal. 'As if he cares.'

'Yeah, he does. Nigil watches you both,' said Torin as he held a piece of hollow metal over his shoulder, his biceps taut and bulging. 'You'd be a big loss to the House, but not irreplaceable.'

'You going to put that on your costume? You can barely lift it?' said Zarifah. She swallowed hard trying not to think about what other part of Torin's body she would like to see bulging.

'Didn't find much, had to pick up something.' He winked back making her think that maybe he had indeed found something of value, enough to keep it a secret. *Maybe a crystal?*

They were scanned at the door to make sure they hadn't picked up any bacteria. The microscopic bugs that multiplied in the dump were enough to make you sick for a week or even kill you. Nigil didn't want his dancers sick and unable to harvest. A Sentinel stood blocking the way after they had been processed and given the green light to go inside the House.

'There's been a delivery.' A tall Sentinel approached Zarifah. 'The Collector wants you now.'

Course he does. He always wants me. Zarifah reluctantly followed the Sentinel to Nigil's office, loosening her clothes that were beginning to suffocate her. *Course he wants me. He always wants me. If only I could stick a knife in his heart and run the bloody place myself.* She no longer knew whether to be happy about new deliveries or not, but she prayed to Her that they would be healthy and not too young.

The young girl, around sixteen but looked more like a child under ten, stood quivering in Nigil's office.

'Do you think that she can dance?' he asked.

How could The Collector could run the House and still not be able to determine if the deliveries could dance or not. Nigil was an emotional like her, and enslaved, but lacked any great skill. His ability was with running a House and collecting high yielding harvests each night.

Part of her soul cried and her heart bled as she looked into the child's honey coloured eyes that spoke of recent horrors endured.

'Well?' Nigil asked impatiently.

'She has the skill but she will need lessons.' Zarifah had

learnt not to lie. She wasn't sure if this delicate girl would last long. She was thin, her wrists showed terrible scars and her soul weak. 'She may not survive the soul split.'

'Take her to the Alchemists.' The girl didn't struggle as she was hauled into the next room by the Sentinel. But then she didn't know what was about to be done to her.

'Productive scavenge?' asked Nigil as they waited. Zarifah shook her head. Her new flowers began to itch against the heavy layers of clothes. She tried to prepare herself, not that it would matter. The screaming always made her knees buckle.

The girl screamed a lot. Zarifah couldn't help herself and held her hands to her ears to try to block out the noise. It sounded like they were trying to cut the girl in half and in a sense they were, just her soul. Nigil took pleasure watching Zarifah's discomfort and she looked away from his grey stare.

The Sentinel carried the girl in his arms as he walked back into the room. The process never took long, but was always horrendous to those who could dance and felt like a life time passed each time another soul was split and imprisoned.

'Etana's in your care. Teach her to dance. You have a month.' Nigil signalled for them to leave as he returned to his record keeping.

Zarifah led the way back to her room and motioned for the Sentinel to lay Etana on her bed. The girl immediately curled into a ball, her back to Zarifah, and sobbed.

Zarifah knelt and stroked the girl's dark thick hair. Her wrists and ankles were bruised badly from where she'd been strapped to the machine. Zarifah remembered when she had been processed. The images that formed in her mind as her soul was divided fuelled repeating nightmares ever since.

Zarifah had believed her father was giving her a surprise for her sixth birthday. But the soul split wasn't what she'd counted on. She stood, still clothed in pants and shirt like a boy in Nigil's room while her father settled his debts and broke her heart. Since she could remember she had been part of her father's crew and travelled around the outer planets trading with whatever would help them survive. *No life for a girl*, he had mumbled to her. But she didn't understand what he meant. When one of the ship members tried to coax her into his room, her father had nearly killed the man. But then he had nearly killed her by selling her to Nigil's house. If only her mother had been there. But her father wouldn't speak of the mother she never knew. She had learnt to live without them both.

Her father had placed his hand on her head as if to say sorry, as he walked from the room leaving Nigil's hungry eyes on the fresh dancer. She had screamed for her mother when her soul had been split, that part of herself she didn't know was there, the part that was uniquely hers and should never have been divided. Her body had thrashed in protest and the cords around her wrists and ankles cut deep into her young flesh.

Zarifah was placed in the care of Atira, the Soul Dancer she replaced. Atira had taught Zarifah everything she knew including the harshness of life in the House. She fell in love with the goddess Her, and finally felt she had come home. The line of the goddess had run deep in her veins and Zarifah didn't need a lot of teaching to bring out what was instinctively part of her soul. The goddess Her became like a mother. It made it easy for Zarifah to vow to do her part in starting the uprising between the soul dancers and the Regulators. Tears streamed down her cheeks as she looked at Etana. *I will stop this.*

5

Etana's body twitched involuntarily as her mind desperately sought comfort. Her soul crystal glowed a soft yet menacing red as the newly imprisoned soul fought for freedom. This fight wouldn't last long and she worried Etana's soul might surrender to death. She sensed the girl's soul pain. The lingering ripples pulsed the familiar grief to her own soul and tears flowed. Even though part of Zarifah's soul was caged, she could still feel, just not as much. She craved for the emotions, strong, bold, good, bad, all of them, to pulse in her body once more, in full strength.

'I'm sorry,' said Zarifah softly as she touched the soul crystal around Etana's neck while she slept, dark patches already haunting her face. 'I will help you.' The promise echoed emptily around the room, because in this underworld the only thing you could be sure about was that there were no guarantees. The most she could do at the moment was to keep the girl in her room. If she helped the girl as much as she could then maybe she would have one more person standing against the Regulators, and an ally for the rebellious plan that Her had told her about.

When Zarifah felt that the girl's soul had surrendered but not given up, she left her to sleep off the real nightmare that had been imprinted on her innocent mind, to check on the afternoon trainings.

'Watch her,' said Zarifah to the Sentinel outside her door. *Nigil doesn't trust me.* She shivered at the thought. She planned to be back before the girl woke. She didn't want the girl to self-harm. It happened often enough after the splitting process. *I had tried.* There were still times when she wished that she had succeeded.

Zarifah hurried to the training room along the grimy corridors, quiet because the dancers, the majority of people in the House were practising.

Torin stood at the front instructing the younger dancers, three boys of various abilities and four girls, around thirteen years old. They weren't ready to perform, but Nigil expected them to have been trained in the basic skill within a few months. Zarifah had tried, with Torin's help, to show them the love of Her, to show that there was some hope.

'Keep your knees bent slightly,' instructed Torin. 'Feel the drum beat.' A hard task for them to do with part of their soul held in an icy prison. Not one of them had a smile, nor looked like they were enjoying themselves.

Zarifah didn't want to teach them how to smell the different emotions, not now as her stomach moaned for food and her mind for sleep and her soul for freedom. *Not like this.*

In the past their skill was revered and celebrated and that's what Zarifah wanted to bring back.

'Will she be any good?' asked Hayal. Her bare midriff showed off the tattooed spiders.

'Maybe,' answered Zarifah with a blank face as she scanned the students trying to mimic Torin's hip movements. 'You've been training too?'

'Yeah.' Hayal placed her hands on her hips. 'I'm one of the best dancers here.'

'The time will come when you may need to take my place.' Zarifah stepped close to Hayal and grabbed her arm tight. 'Make sure you are ready, for if you're not as skilled as me, Nigil, or another Collector, may cast you out and find another.'

Hayal bowed her head.

'You are replaceable.' Zarifah frowned. 'No matter how good you are.' She let go of Hayal, who rubbed her arm. Her own words rippled with a chill. *I'm replaceable too.*

Zarifah clapped her hands and the dancers gathered around. The younger members had a small shine of respect for the Soul Dancer, the other members had sheer hate and hunger for her position. They were all like animals and their primal urges for survival at all costs pulsed from their bodies in a pungent smell of hate and fear weakened by their entrapped souls. How she wished she had hope and could free them. But some of them didn't believe in Her and only danced because they were forced to. *I should tell them a story and remind them of what it was like.* She clenched her jaw with determination. *It will be like that again.*

'Jarah you need to work on your body ripples, your stomach is starting to hang over your belt,' said Zarifah as she scanned the dancers. Some of the more experienced dancers weren't there and she was angry they would skip training. The harvesting dance was so specific for each species that came in as patrons, they needed to always be ready.

'Dahra, your costumes need to be changed, you've used that one for the last month, the patrons want to see something different.' Her words were like whips sending out stinging reminders of what their prison bars looked like. They might be part of the underworld, but there were standards to maintain.

'Hayal, you were too slow in your extractions.' Hayal glared back defiantly at the criticism.

'You're too harsh,' interrupted Nigil as he entered the room.

'I though you wanted me to ensure the dancers can perform their best so they can bring in high yields.' She folded her arms across her chest. *I'm not going to take his crap today.*

'The new one still alive?' he asked. He strode up to Zarifah.

'Barely,' answered Zarifah. Her skin prickled. *Something is going on.* He didn't come to practices unless he needed to berate the dancers.

'I have a patron.' Nigil's face remained blank but held the sort of arrogance that had helped him to get this position. His grey eyes held her own and she forced herself not to look away.

Zarifah clenched her hands tight to stop herself from

reacting. She forced herself to look at Nigil and not glance over to Torin. *Please no, Her, please don't let him make me perform in one of the rooms upstairs.*

'He's willing.' Zarifah's heart pulsed a little quicker knowing that Nigil was presenting something that would be considered risky for the House.

'Why not tell him to come back tonight? That's when this sort of business is done.' She spat the words at Nigil.

Nigil's eyebrows knotted together and a shadow cast over his face. 'Don't ask me why.'

'Owe him, do you?' She couldn't help it. The words filtered out of her dry mouth before her mind could stop them. She'd been playing this game too long with Nigil and today she'd had enough, especially with Torin standing nearby, watching.

'Don't you dare.' His voice icy cold and his eyes narrowed with anger. The look he wore was one that she'd seen many times before. Right before being whipped.

I'm right. But that didn't matter. The soul crystal pulsed around her neck reminding Zarifah of her position here. 'Okay,' she answered, her voice cool and controlled. *What choice do I have?* She didn't want to endure another beating. *I have to choose my battles.* A dance wouldn't hurt her.

Nigil stepped close to Zarifah and lowered his voice. 'Oh no, I don't mean for you to perform.'

Zarifah stomach roiled. *Whatever he has in mind I'm not going to like it.*

'I have a patron for your students to practise on.' Nigil

glanced around the room, the dancers looked at the ground not wanting to meet his eyes. 'It's time more of you were dancing.'

'But the stage needs to be set,' said Zarifah, scrambling to find a reason to say no. 'There won't be enough time without interfering with tonight's performance.'

'There will be plenty of time. So who do you think should have the honour of their first harvest?' Nigil turned to face the younger students.

'Stop, you are making them nervous,' interrupted Zarifah. She could take his abuse, but not on the younglings, not yet, and not before one of them was about to perform the harvest for the first time.

'Jarah is ready.' Zarifah selected the most experience dancers who hadn't performed. At sixteen she'd been holding him back hoping that Jarah wouldn't have to dance like this, hoping that she'd succeed by bringing back Her and starting an uprising. But she hadn't managed any of this yet. *No wonder Her is angry with me.*

'Are you ready?' Nigil towered over Jarah.

'I'm ready.' Jarah squared his shoulders but his voice wavered.

Nigil straightened his back. 'You have an hour to get ready. The others can watch, it will be good for their learning.'

Zarifah stepped in front of Nigil to stop him from leaving. 'What if he fails?' she whispered. She had a disastrous scene forming in her mind. The last thing she needed was for a student to fail. Without the goddess residing on Earth there was less talent in harvesting and with the conflict between the Emotionless they needed to nurture those who had the talent of Her pulsing in their blood.

'I have a bullet ready. The man might have won his bet but he signed his death sentence when gambling with me in the first place.' He smiled.

A cold shiver extended through her body.

'Bring Jarah.'

Zarifah lowered her head in obedience and waited for Nigil to leave. His shoes, shiny and black, clipped on the polished concrete floor, causing her heart to thunder fast and hard. *He's gone too far this time.*

'Torin get Jarah ready. Hayal and Dahra will also dance with you, but you will *not* complete any extractions, he must do this himself.' Zarifah wrinkled her forehead. *This isn't going to end well.* She hated not being able to change the situation and protect the dancers. *Her forgive me.*

'I will lose a chance for payment dance tonight if I dance now,' said Hayal. 'Choose someone else.'

'I should dance with him.' Torin placed his hands protectively on the shoulders of the boy.

'No.' Zarifah clenched her jaw in an attempt to control her anger.

'I have the experience to help him without Nigil knowing,' Torin insisted.

'Not today.' Zarifah remained firm. 'I don't want you killed.' She looked into his blue eyes pleading with him silently for him to listen to her. *I can't face being here without you.*

Torin lowered his eyes. 'Fine then.'

Zarifah took a deep breath, her hands trembled and she clasped them together before anyone could see.

'Jarah, Hayal and Dahra get ready, the rest of you are to sit and watch, but make sure you are well away from the patron.' She moved to the more experienced dancers. She looked at Torin and Hayal. 'Take the younglings back to the dorms. Make them stay there.'

Torin nodded his head sharply. 'It will be all right. Jarah will complete the harvest.' He rested his hand on her shoulder. Heat rippled from his hand down into her muscles easing the tension inside of her but building a different sort of tension—desire.

'I hope so.' His hand slipped away. Come back. Zarifah wanted to say the words aloud, to hug him and forget about what was really going on here. But of course she didn't. Her resolve held as Torin ushered the younglings away.

Please Her, keep my dancers safe. They love you, really they do. Zarifah prayed. It was the only thing left that she could do. Nigil had set the stage and they all had to play along. No matter what.

6

'You must harvest what you can, no matter how common an emotion you may find, no matter the species out there.' She looked directly at Jarah as he stood with his back to the curtain, hands high ready to begin moving when the curtain was drawn. He briefly nodded but did he really understand? *Please watch over Jarah.* Zarifah rearranged Jarah's costume for the third time.

'Gentleman, you have the pleasure of a unique performance at The Collector's generosity,' said The Presenter. He tipped his top hat, pushed it in the air, and let it tumble before catching it on his head.

'May Her be with you,' whispered Zarifah. She returned to the side of the stage and watched. Her fingers twisted at a metal chain hanging around her waist.

His bare chest was toned, but his young body hadn't filled out. He was like a ripening piece of fruit, too early to taste just yet. But some patrons liked that. Zarifah prayed the harvest would be something not so dark, maybe curiosity with its after rain smell, nothing too negative which could cause damage to his mind. The darker emotions seemed to remind the part of the soul trapped in the crystal of what it was missed.

He wore tight black plastic pants, which tightened his buttocks so they looked like they were ready to burst. There were a few chains looped around his belt and along his long arms. He didn't have a tattoo. Jarah had to pass this test first, and then he might graduate to be a dancer, but only if Nigil was pleased. *At least he is of age at sixteen.* Still Zarifah wished he was performing his first harvest under different circumstances, like such dances were meant to be performed back before the Regulators took over. This dance was sacred and used to heal people of grief, fear and anger to enhance their own joy.

Torin stood protectively behind Etana, as if her new Sentinel. Her eyes were glazed and it looked like she'd been given a pill. *Torin would've thought of something like that.*

The drums began to sound out a soft slow beat. Zarifah's blood rushed in anticipation of the desire to harvest.

Zarifah stood out of sight but able to see the performance. *Her, keep him safe.*

'Drink, to the show!' The Presenter strode from the stage.

Zarifah took a deep breath, hoping to detect a sign of emotion Jarah would be extracting. Even from this distance she had the skill to find emotion that could be harvested. But there was nothing. No spicy scent of happiness, not even grief or jealously. The thought of failure punched through her mind. *No. Her, watch over Jarah.*

Jarah's body moved gracefully around the stage commanding attention from the patron.

Zarifah stopped her body from twitching with the drums, her body yearned to move with the music, and her heart wanted to help Jarah. She couldn't complete the harvest from this distance but she could always start the harvest dance and direct her energy towards the patron and tease out the emotions. But then she wouldn't be able to dance tonight. And Nigil would punish her. *I could endure a beating to save Jarah.*

She inhaled, trying to detect any emotion from the patron. A faint smell, putrid and rotting, worse than the smell of the garbage they had sorted through this morning. The emotion disgust wafted towards the stage and her nose tingled. Her knees weakened a little when she saw Jarah move towards the patron. Another alien. *An Icehon.* Anyone was welcome down here at the Wolf House.

Dark green gas, only seen by the dancers, snaked out from the mouth of the Icehon towards the collecting crystals around Jarah's neck.

Go slow. Jarah moved too fast. Zarifah held her breath knowing he wasn't likely to succeed now. Before she could step up to the stage herself and assist the inexperience dancer, Hayal pushed past her.

Zarifah stumbled. 'What are you doing?' Hayal ignored her. *Stupid girl.*

Before she'd righted her balance another dancer, Dahra began dancing and joined them. *I'm going to whip both of them.* She clenched her jaw tight as the two dancers join Jarah. They were both good dancers and she didn't want anything untoward to happen to them. She didn't want to lose Jarah either but then he hadn't proved himself, and as untested talent he was dispensable. They weren't.

Hayal's dancing slowed Jarah down. He instinctively circled the Icehonian. The blue blood in the alien's neck pulsed a darker colour of pleasure. Zarifah held her breath. *Maybe.* She dared not wish for the impossible too soon. The tension in the room made the air heavy. *Relax. This could go horribly wrong.*

The bluish skin of the Icehon illuminated more green in the soft lights and Jarah made deliberate movements trying to entice the alien's eyes to drink in his body.

Zarifah felt a part of herself merge with Jarah. He began to ripple his toned stomach muscles, up and down, up and down, gracefully and slowly. The alien's eyes glazed over. Nearly half an hour had past and Zarifah could sense the boy was tired. His hands began their own dance around the body of the Icehon trying to find the source of the disgust.

The alien's oversized belly vibrated with the beats of the drum. Not the most pleasant creature to want to complete an extraction on. But Jarah didn't recoil. He stepped between the legs of the Icehon, inhaling deeply as if breathing the emotion upwards towards the small oblong head of the Icehon.

Zarifah expected to see the dark shades of the energy of the emotion disgust flow from the mouth of the alien, but nothing happened. She saw the muscles in Jarah's neck tighten, his veins stood out as he repeated the movement with his body pushing up against the patron. Each emotion had a distinct odour, but only those trained in the skills of the soul dancers could detect the different scents.

Don't give up. Icehons were stubborn creatures and Jarah would have to be patient. The strain was beginning to form on the young dancer's face. *Keep going.*

Jarah straddled the alien and wrapped his legs around its ample waist. With strong muscles from training he held his weight as he leaned into the alien. Jarah pressed his lips onto the patron's mouth.

A moan escaped from the Icehon. A deep guttural moan of pleasure. Zarifah breathed in sharply. A black gas floated out from the patron. He moved his arms guiding the gas to the collecting crystals around his neck. Slowly the emotion of disgust weakened as the harvest drew to a close.

Stop now. But Jarah kept his mouth on the alien's. *Jarah!* Zarifah stepped forward, but a hand gripped her arm. She turned to see Torin. He shook his head. She looked back towards the dance. Jarah was still going, and there was no more emotion to be harvested. She clenched her jaw. *Please help him, Her.* Torn between wanting to stop this before Jarah lost himself with the soul of the alien and knowing that there was nothing she could do, because he had to sever the connection himself.

A single beat of the drum echoed in the room. The sound turned on something in the young dancer. Suddenly, Jarah pulled away from the alien.

Zarifah exhaled and Torin let go of her arm.

Jarah stumbled away from the patron before collapsing exhausted. Hayal and Dahra rushed to help him.

Nigil stepped forward.

'Great performance.' The Icehon smiled, his eyes glazed.

'You got more than you deserved,' spoke Nigil with an edge to his voice.

'I want more of that.'

'Debt is settled.' Nigil moved around the alien, breathing purposefully; Zarifah held her breath. *Was there an emotion Jarah missed? Or is there something else that could have been harvested tonight?* She breathed in deeply. A hint of spiciness filled her lungs. *Fuck.* Somehow Jarah had stirred happiness in the patron. *Probably because the heavier emotion of disgust had been removed.* It happened sometimes. She inhaled again. Her mind fogged at the edges at the chance of tasting happiness. Her knees weakened a little as her desire welled deep within her. *I want that emotion.* It pushed away all her fears and worries. *Happiness.*

'Looks like there's still some harvesting to do.' Nigil signalled for the drums to start again and he moved towards the dancers. 'Hayal you may have the honour of this dance.'

Hayal didn't need a second invitation. She left Jarah and moved with the rhythm of the drums sliding seductively across the floor towards the Icehon.

'No.' Zarifah could only manage a whisper. Just the smell of happiness wafting from the alien had stirred the memory of the other night. It opened a hole of emptiness within her and she struggled to keep her mind clear. *This should be my dance as Soul Dancer.* She looked at Nigil. He raised an eyebrow at her then returned his attention to the Hayal as she sat on the patron's lap. *He's baiting me.* She held her breath, not trusting herself at what would happen if she breathed in the spicy joy. *Keep calm.* Zarifah pressed her fingernails into her palms, sharp pain kept her mind clear. *Don't show him how much I want this.*

Hayal stood up and parted the legs of the alien and swayed her hips in a continuous figure of eight. His eyes glazed over. The smell of cinnamon intensified. A deep rich colour of pink in a gas-like form eased out of his mouth. She moved her hands, slow and heavy as if they were in water and directed the emotion to the collecting crystals around her neck.

Jealousy spiked within Zarifah. She dug her fingers in her palms harder. *I should be doing that.*

Hayal severed the connection with a passionate kiss; her hands held his head tight as her lips covered his. She pulled away with a smile that sickened Zarifah. *She will not take my position.*

He clasped his hands around her hips and buried his head between her breasts, forcing his long tongue under the material of her costume.

Nigil held up a gun and fired. Hayal screamed as the brains of the alien splattered over her. The alien's body collapsed, dead, nearly crushing her. Torin rushed forward, with the other male dancers and lifted the dead alien off Hayal.

'You were getting too friendly with my dancers. I don't like that.' Nigil put away the gun. 'You're in my debt now.'

'This is why we don't do private dances,' said Zarifah as she ran out from the side of the stage to help the Hayal who sat stunned on the floor covered in blue blood and pieces of alien brain.

'No this is exactly what we do.' Nigil stood over the dead alien. His shoulders square and back stiff straight. 'I don't tolerate anyone taking advantage of me.' He glanced at Zarifah, his grey gaze sent shivers down her back. She forced herself to hold his eyes. *He can't know what I've got planned.* But doubt restricted her breath. *No he can't. I've been careful.*

'His pod and money will help our House with the trade and new supplies. You.' He pointed to a Sentinel. 'Clean up this mess. Rest of you have two seconds to leave otherwise I'll be using more bullets.'

7

'Get up.' The Sentinel shook Zarifah. She had wrapped her body around Etana and had barely slept having to share her narrow bed with another. 'The Regulators are here, they want to inspect the House.'

'Fuck,' whispered Zarifah. The Regulators carried out random inspections, but them coming after a patron was murdered made her think the two events were connected. She shook Etana. 'You have to get up.'

'No, no, no, go away,' Etana began to yell.

'If you don't things could get worse for you,' coaxed Zarifah as she struggled to lift the thrashing girl from the bed.

'No. No.' The girl screamed louder. The crystal holding part of her soul pulsed with a blood red colour.

'Do you have something for her?' she asked the Sentinel desperately.

'No, and you know the rules. Not when the Regulators are here. They will take more than her if they had evidence of substance use.' The big man stood blocking the doorway. Zarifah hoped Nigil could negotiate out of this one.

Zarifah slapped the girl, weakly. It had an effect. Etana sobbed into her hands. 'You will behave.'

Etana looked at her with red and swollen eyes. *I have to make her understand.*

'You don't want the Regulators to pick you out. If you're crying I won't be able to help you.' Zarifah held the girl's shoulders and looked into her eyes. 'Do you understand? I'm helping you.'

Etana nodded weakly. 'Good. You make sure that you do what you're told. And no tears.' She hoped the Regulators wouldn't take Etana to feed from her emotions. It would leave the girl too weak after having her soul split. *Stupid Nigil. He always fucked things up for the dancers here. All for his own gain.* Zarifah quickly wiped Etana's face and tied back her hair.

'Quick now.' Zarifah held Etana's hand tightly as they walked to the training room.

Members of the Wolf House stood in silence in ordered lines. Some looked half asleep, others angry at the disruption, and most smelt of fear. The Regulators in their deathly grey uniforms, pants, shirt and small yet powerful laser guns, had begun looking for drugs or any signs of worship to Her.

Zarifah squeezed Etana's hand reassuringly and pushed into the group of dancers close to Torin and Hayal. She pulled the Etana close.

'Don't cry, don't look scared, don't talk,' Zarifah spoke

softly but commandingly in the girl's ear before scanning the room to see if she could determine what was happening.

The room smelt of fear, the acidic sharpness caused Zarifah to wrinkle her nose. There was a hint of citrus, faint and out of place in the room. The tell-tale sign of surprise. Even the people with part of their souls enslaved involuntarily sent out odours of their emotions. The Regulators absorbed the emotional energy.

Etana squeezed her hand, struggling to stand. 'They'll be gone soon.' Zarifah's own emotions pulled away from her body leaving her light-headed.

The black emotionless eyes of the Regulators made Zarifah's stomach flip, but she kept their empty gaze as each of them walked past her.

One Regulator paused at Etana. 'She's been given something.' His voice monotone sounded harsh. 'Collector that will be 10 emotions.'

Zarifah swallowed hard. That's a lot of emotion. She wasn't sure Nigil would be able to pay. She held her breath and prayed. *Please don't let them want personal feeding sessions.*

'The girl has just been crying,' said Nigil calmly. He fidgeted with his tie. 'She's new, came in this morning and is still fighting the effects of the process.'

'Fifteen emotions.'

'Surely, there's another...'

'Twenty.' The Regulator moved on, systematically looking closely at each dancer in the line.

'Let's go to my office and sort out payment,' suggested

Nigil. His sweaty smell, a mix of aniseed and testosterone intensified.

'If anyone leaves this room they will be shot,' said the Regulator as they walked away.

Guarded by five Regulators, the members of the Wolf House shifted uneasily and waited in silence. No one talked or sat down on the concrete floor. They would have to start getting ready for the nightly performance soon. Zarifah caught Torin looking at her. Warmth spread out around her. He smiled quickly, a brief reassurance, then looked away.

The longer Zarifah waited, the more nervous she became. She twisted the edge of the material of her loose pants. *This isn't a good sign. If only Nigil hadn't gotten greedy.* Usually the House had to pay fines, but somehow they managed to keep some emotions for illegal trade, otherwise they would be swallowing nutrient pills for the next few months.

Nigil looked visibly annoyed when he returned nearly an hour later. 'We have a performance tonight, get ready.' He clapped his hands, his forehead wrinkled with concern, and he strode out of the room. 'The Regulators want a feast.'

The dancers rushed to their rooms to freshen up for the performance.

'I hate dancing for the Regulators,' said Zarifah quietly to Torin as they walked along the corridor. Etana walked by her side, eyes wide with fear. It was difficult to produce enough emotions to feed the Regulators when half of her soul was imprisoned in a crystal. The teardrop crystal pulsed warm on her skin.

'It's going to take a lot of focus,' said Torin. 'But we've done this before.'

'I'm...' She walked close to Torin feeling his heat, causing her head to blur and a hint of cinnamon wafted between them. His effect on her was getting more difficult to ignore.

'Get moving,' said a Sentinel as his words whipped the dancers around them moving quicker.

'What about Jarah?' said Torin.

'He'll be fine, hopefully,' said Zarifah as she tried to focus on working out something that would untangle this current mess. 'Send him here, he could watch the girl while we dance.'

'Move along,' yelled an oversized Sentinel.

'You be careful.' He brushed his fingers casually along her lower back leaving a trail of heat that weakened Zarifah's knees. He turned quickly before she could stop him and do something that she would end up regretting.

Zarifah rushed into her room. 'Fuck.' She paused at the doorway looking at the mess. Most of her costumes lay on the floor. Her room would have to be put back together later. Cursing, Zarifah settled Etana in her bed then quickly freshened up. She twisted red shiny material around her breasts and tied the ends behind her neck and added black strips of material around her waist, then slipped on a slim belt full of copper discs dangling from strategic places around her belly.

She rearranged her hair into long plaits and secured them in a ponytail. *Her, give me strength.* She paused to catch her breath and to try and think. But a knock at the door forced her back into action.

Zarifah pressed the button to open the electric door and Jarah, clothed in loose blue harem pants and tight matching coloured t-shirt stood looking at the ground.

'Soul Dancer, you asked for me.' His voice trembled.

'Come in.' He needed some support but the sight of him reminded her of his failure and the danger in which he had placed Hayal and Dahra.

'You're to watch the girl.' She tied matching strings of copper discs in her hair. Her plaits tickled her bare skin on her lower back.

'Yes, Soul Dancer.' He looked at his feet.

Zarifah pursed her lips together. Unsure whether they should be left here. But her room was a better option than the stage, and since Jarah had performed today already he wouldn't have much emotion to help feed the Regulators and she wanted to keep Etana away from the stage for as long as she could. She rushed to the stage. *Her, watch them both.*

Fifteen dancers gathered side stage, a nervous silence vibrated between them.

Zarifah slowly moved around the dancers organising them into groups and reminded them that they only had to do a primal dance tonight and to be ready for changes at the last minute. No one questioned her so she supposed that they had guessed.

'Are the younglings in the dormitories?' she asked Torin.

'Yes Soul Dancer,' he answered.

'Thank you.' She squeezed his hand secretly and was

relieved to feel him return the pressure, grateful to have his support.

She looked through the peephole at the side of the stage and saw Nigil sitting with the Regulators acting as if they were his best mates, laughing and slapping them on their backs. They sat in the middle and there weren't many patrons tonight. Most would take one look at the Regulators and simply leave and go to the next House. People of the underworld kept away from the authorities, a fundamental rule. But tonight they would be dancing to produce their own emotions for the Regulators to consume. *I hope we can feed them.*

The Presenter stepped onto the stage, twirling his cane. Zarifah went back to ensure that the first group of dancers were ready.

'Tonight's dancers will make your skin tingle,' said The Presenter. His words slipped from Zarifah's mind as she looked over the costumes of the dancers before standing at the side of the stage.

'Enjoy!' And there was an eruption of whistles and hooting as the curtains parted.

Three dancers started the evening's performance. Metal chains clinked as they moved together trying to bring their own emotions to the surface and then send the energy to the Regulators. It was the harvest in reverse, almost.

'Do you think we'll be fed?' asked Torin from behind Zarifah. His hand brushed down her spine sending a multitude of electric waves over her body.

'I pray so.' Her voice soft. She focused her attention back

to the stage, ignoring the fired flaming inside of her from the lingering touch.

The dancers worked hard on the stage. Hips snapped with the drumbeats, urging the emotions to surface. A lot of bitterness hung in the air, along with the red emotional gas of anger, which flowed to the Regulators, directed by the movements of the dancers.

The Regulators sat and drank, absorbing any emotion that was around the room from other patrons. Group after group of dancers went out to hypnotise the crowd with their bodies. Zarifah sensed the Regulators fill with anger. *They need to feed on something else.* She swallowed hard. She didn't want the Regulators to anger. *I have to try to produce curiosity or surprise.* She'd much rather have the emotion happiness coursing through her, but she doubted that she could produce such an emotion in this situation.

'There's one more dance, one that you won't be able to resist.' The words of The Presenter became intense. 'The Soul Dancer.'

Torin grabbed Zarifah by the arm and dragged her to the stage just as the curtains were drawn once again. Without even looking at each other they posed their bodies.

This isn't a good idea. Smoke bellowed around their ankles like lost clouds.

Her back to the crowd, she began to snake her arms up from her hips to above her head. Stretching slowly and deliberately between the beats of the drums, she kept her body still as only her arms rippled like the muscles of the snake, to the left and then back again. Torin stood still and she could hear him slowing down his breathing to be in time with hers.

With her arms reaching above her head she moved her hips around as if there was a ball of energy to play with. Her hips changed direction so that the ball rolled upwards. Then her ribs moved the ball of seductive energy around before sending the invisible ball back down to her hips. She repeated this movement as she arched her shoulders and arms. She turned to face the audience.

Concentrating hard, she pushed the ball of energy back and forth between her hips. Torin stretched his arms out towards her. His muscular stomach pulsed with her moving hips as he began to create his own ball of energy.

They both danced in time with each other, mesmerising the crowd. With each movement the individual balls of energy became intense and they became closer, bringing their own emotions to the surface.

Torin's breathing was heavy and controlled. He stood behind her, his larger body almost protectively framing hers as she rolled her energy ball up and down between her hips and breasts and his arms floated around her assets, fingering the strands of metal like harp strings.

In a slow spin they faced each other and joined their balls of energy and held each other close. Energy spread between them, seeping out and creating a new ball for them to play with. The scent of cinnamon drifted between them. A faint smell only detectable by those trained in the manipulation of emotions; an emotion that could only be produced in honesty, when there was trust, and not something that could be faked. A rarity. The emotion filled the emptiness inside of Zarifah. Her movements were less laboured, and joy buzzed around her, clouding her mind with a hint of bliss. *I want more.*

With one leg around his waist, she contracted her thigh muscles for support and arched backwards, begging him to follow. He bent down and kissed above her belly button and moved upwards as if pulling her back. But just as their lips were about to find each other, they spun around, holding each other tight, begging the other to lose control first.

He rolled his body down along hers, rotating the ball of happiness between them and then back up. Down and up they moved, stretching the tension in the ball they had created.

Embracing, they could resist no more and she leant backwards, slightly. He found her mouth and they kissed. The ball burst. A cinnamon scent rippled out from their touch. Zarifah had never had a kiss like this before. *A real kiss.* One that was sacred between two who had feelings for each other. Torin's tenderness for her exploded with pleasant heat on her lips and she played her tongue over his not allowing the kiss to stop. He moved with her motion, sucking gently at her lips. He hardened beneath her touch and she stifled a groan. A little kiss had opened an entire new world for her and she trembled inside, knowing that it was going to be difficult to ignore him.

The drums stopped. The deep pink coloured gas flowed

to the Regulators. They absorbed the ripples, hungrily and wanting more.

8

Zarifah and the other dancers stood on the stage like herded animals ready to be selected.

'I'll take these two,' said the Regulator in charge. He'd selected two of the male dancers. He was directed away with the dancers to the upstairs rooms and the other Regulators began to grab who they wanted.

Zarifah kept looking ahead, trying not to engage with any of the Regulators. *Please don't pick Torin.* But that was inevitable. Just like she was going to be taken away to the private rooms.

'Her.' A young Regulator pointed to Hayal. She stumbled a little as she walked behind the man towards the spiral staircase off to the right of the bar area.

Zarifah barely noticed the female Regulator standing in front of her, a blank face unable to show any sort of human emotion.

'You.' The female Regulator, tall and muscular, pointed at Zarifah.

Zarifah turned and walked from the room. She caught Nigil's glance. He winked at Zarifah. *Bastard*. He didn't have to have his emotions sucked from him. Hate and anger burned in her belly as she fixed her gaze on the back of the Sentinel who was taking them to a room. She tried to prepare herself for the vacuuming of her emotions by the Regulator.

Because of her status, Zarifah was given one of the more comfortable and well decorated rooms upstairs. Small electric candles had been turned on and placed around the room, setting a seductive mood. There were large cushions in the centre of the room next to a table with a flask and two small cups.

'Liquor?' Zarifah asked trying not to sound nervous. Each new client took some getting used to, to discover what pleasure they really wanted. *Maybe I'll just dance*. But the emptiness in the female suggested that she wanted to absorb as much emotional energy from Zarifah as possible.

'No, come here.' The Regulator settled herself on the cushions. Zarifah moved close and waited for more instructions. The woman's strong hands guided Zarifah next to her. She read the name Senara on her uniform.

'Tell me, what's it like to have emotions?' The question tugged in Zarifah's mind. This wasn't what she was usually asked in these rooms. Things more like "What are you willing to do for another pill?" or if she was lucky, a patron would tempt her with the prospect of another flower, but she'd learnt that they didn't always come through with their promises.

'What's it like not to have emotions?' Zarifah asked back. The Regulator's face remained unchanged. Zarifah hated the scentless body next to her.

'Easy,' Senara answered.

Suddenly the Regulator's hands were around Zarifah's neck. She gasped for breath.

'Oh yes, fear, with a pinch of surprise,' moaned Senara, her grip firm. 'But your captured soul weakens your emotions.' She pressed harder. 'I want more.'

Fear flowed from Zarifah's body and straight into the body of the woman. The rotting smell filled the room briefly before being consumed by Senara. Then another wave of fear gripped Zarifah. Senara fed on the emotion.

'Delicious.' The Regulator released her grip. Zarifah coughed as she tried to breathe but the woman settled her heavier body over hers.

'Let's see what other emotions I can take from you.' The Regulator began a different approach. She traced her fingers along the bare skin of Zarifah's face.

Zarifah responded under the delicate touch. A citrus fragrance hinted in the air, curiosity oozed from Zarifah as the Regulator traced around the outline of the red material covering her breasts. Somehow the citrus odour lingered in the air around Zarifah, building in intensity. After nearly being strangled, such tenderness lulled Zarifah into the secure feeling of comfort.

The Regulator kept her fingers moving in a slow, sensual

rhythm and held herself back from absorbing the emotions. The tension between the women hummed. Senara's fingers moved further down, leaving no part of Zarifah's exposed skin untouched. Both longed for pleasure and happiness, only one could produce such an emotion and the other could only receive such an emotion. But their lives were too dark, and neither was capable of producing anything spicy.

Zarifah glided her fingers down the cool skin of the Regulator parting her thighs and slipping over the harsh material of her uniform.

Senara reached up and ran her hand down Zarifah's face. Zarifah nearly lost her rhythm. This wasn't what she was used to. *I'm the one who gives pleasure.* The Regulator moved her hand down, tracing Zarifah's collarbone and then brushed over her breast. She tugged at the red material and pulled it away. Zarifah struggled to keep focus on giving to her client. She unbuckled Senara's trousers and slipped her fingers over her mound, then in between her fleshy folds, already thick with moisture. Zarifah plunged her fingers inside and was rewarded with a sharp gasp. Senara found Zarifah's breast with her mouth and played her tongue over her hardening nipple. They pleasured the other, until neither could produce or receive any more and with a soft gasp they released and collapsed back down into the cushions as the ripples of the citrus scent faded into the Regulator.

Zarifah breathed hard. To settle herself she reached over to pour her client a glass of Spirit and some for herself.

'This could become a habit.' Senara sipped at the liquid, as if this was what she normally would do as part of her job, her other hand fondled Zarifah's breast. This would be one client who could be on her always-to-see list. A habit that maybe she could learn to enjoy. The longer she lay next to the female, the more nausea engulfed her for allowing such an emotion to have been elicited, and from an Emotionless. *I could use her to help me complete my belt, to earn my freedom.* Then Her's work can be done. Zarifah's skin prickled.

Thoughts rolled through her mind as she forgot her life here at the House, how she'd broken so many of the teachings of the goddess, but her thoughts muddled as the female started the process again and her body surrendered immediately, enjoying the chance to escape.

***

'Zarifah!' The voice at the door commanded her awake. She untangled herself from Senara who also stirred from sleep. She draped the red material around her naked body and opened the door a little to see who was disturbing her.

'Time's up.' A Sentinel stood in the doorway.

The words bought Zarifah back to her reality. 'Of course.' She turned back into the room to gather the rest of her costume that was scattered around the room.

Senara dressed and became her captor once more. Her cold dark eyes showed nothing of the pleasure or the curiosity she had eaten during the night.

'Have I pleased you?' Zarifah lowered her eyes. A heavy feeling in her stomach turned making her think that maybe she was going to miss getting any sort of payment tonight. *I just want the flowers on my belt.*

'Maybe I'll see you again.' Senara kissed Zarifah, pushing a payment under the dancer's tongue. She pulled away slowly sucking at Zarifah's bottom lip. Then she turned and left.

Zarifah turned the package over in her mouth with her tongue as she walked back to her room. Whatever it was she hoped it would numb the feeling of having to entertain like this, especially for not getting any flowers for her tattoo.

Back in her room, Zarifah woke Jarah from a mess of blankets on the floor. Her tongue had absently played with the payment, which she would only look at when alone. That was going to be difficult with Etana in her care.

'Take her to get food,' she told Jarah. Zarifah pushed the two from her room. Her stomach reminded her that she should really follow them; they only had food once a day, and that was produced from a generator, bland and chemically composed. Nothing grew on the surface; it was too cold and polluted and the underground too hot. They had to rely on machines to make their food.

Besides, after last night, Nigil might be too stingy to even give them food, depending on how much he had to pay to keep the Regulators happy. That was always the purpose of these inspections. For them to feed. *The emotionless bastards.* She looked at her room and the mess they had created. She removed the package from under her tongue. A small container of tiny pills, nutrients, pick me ups. *Useful.*

Swallowing a nutrient pill, she hid the rest in a secret

compartment at the top of her bed. Despite the disturbance to her room it hadn't been discovered.

Zarifah wiped her own sweat and the Regulator's from her body before selecting loose black pants, harem style, with a tight fitting black wrap top, the coolest thing to wear down here in the underground rooms of the House. She banged the air unit, but it still only pumped out warm air, but at least the air was clean. Her room was warm and slightly sticky, a suppressive feeling weighed down on her shoulders.

'Shit!' she moaned as she sat down on her bed and thought of the previous night, ignoring the sewing that she needed to start on now, to ensure she had something to wear tonight.

'How could I?' A faint putrid smell wafted to her nose. The door opened and she knew who it was without having to open her eyes.

'Long night?' asked Torin.

Zarifah looked at her feet not wanting to look him in the eye. It wasn't like this was the first time something like this had happened, besides he had been with a Regulator too, yet uneasiness twisted in her stomach. All because of a kiss they shared. But to Zarifah it was so much more than a kiss. A part of her heart had been unlocked; a part that she wished could be locked again, because now she wanted so much more from Torin. *And I can't have him. Nigil will kill him if he knew.* It was bad enough they kissed on stage in full view. *Nigil will be watching us closely.*

'Your neck. Did something bad happen?' His voice was thick with concern.

Zarifah shook her head. The red marks on her neck were

nothing to be concerned with. On top of the sharp twists in her belly, a burning heat was growing between her thighs and she wasn't sure how to keep all those feelings contained. She wasn't sure that she wouldn't reach up and kiss him again, taste his sweet lips on hers. She pushed the building heat back down stopping herself just in time from acting out any tenderness towards him.

Torin stepped closer. His heat spiked a flush through her. She risked looking up at him. His blue eyes caused her heart to quicken. *We can't.*

Torin stroked his fingers along the side of her head, tucking back a wayward lock of dark hair. Shivers exploded through Zarifah's body. The touch tender, soft, loving, it was so different. *Better then the touch of Senara.*

'Senara was pleased.' Nigil stood in the doorway, arms folded across his chest.

Torin jerked his hand away and stepped from Zarifah. Her stomach twisted in knots of guilt.

Nigil tilted his head. 'Leaving, weren't you?'

Torin left. Zarifah swallowed hard knowing if Nigil didn't say much now he would remember and she would have to pay later. And she would be made to pay. And Torin would too.

'You're reaching new levels which I trust you're teaching to the younglings.' His eyes lingered on the red markings on her neck.

'Yes.' She glared at him.

'Senara indicated she might be back.' She could smell the bitterness from him peppered with anger.

'That's good.' She clenched her jaw. She didn't want to be with Senara, but if it would lead to her tattoos being finished soon then she would endure. 'You should be pleased with that.'

'Not with what I just saw.' Darkness crossed his face. Zarifah held her breath waiting. *He's going to punish me. Slowly.*

'Get the boy to dance tonight, no extractions for him. Make sure he does it or he'll get the same fate as the Icehon.'

'Yes, Collector.'

He grabbed her arm and pulled her violently towards him. The pain in her arm reminded her that she'd been breaking his House rules.

'Don't think I didn't see the kiss between you and Torin.'

A chill went through Zarifah. She struggled to meet his eyes.

Nigil pulled her body into his and kissed her, strongly and passionately, causing her neck backwards awkwardly.

'If you ruin this arrangement with Senara, I'll break something in you.' He fingered her soul crystal. Their breaths mingled with the other's emotions as he kissed her again until she relaxed in his grip, giving him false hope of surrender. This game she knew how to play.

'You're lucky I've got things to do and can't stay.' He held her body. She didn't need to smell his longing to know that he could have her there and then, his body firm under hers.

Nigil released her suddenly and she stumbled as he opened the door.

'Start training Etana today.'

Etana and Jarah stood awkwardly at the door trying to get out of The Collector's way as he left.

'Make sure you learn about dancing quickly.'

Zarifah took a deep breath, watching Nigil walk away. Things were starting to spiral out of control. She couldn't keep the inexperienced dancers safe if they were forced to dance the harvest like this. Her mind whirled through options but kept coming up blank. *Looks like I don't have a choice.*

9

Zarifah's new flowers from the other night itched on her skin reminding her that there were only 24 flowers to go and then she would be free. She corrected Hayal's arms as she walked around the dancers performing a basic routine under Torin's instruction. *It's not like Nigil would really allow me to be free.* But as long as she had the completed belt of flowers around her waist, all one hundred, then she might just get enough bargaining power to start the rebellion against the Regulators and more importantly complete the ritual to bring Her back. And that was another problem. Her wouldn't say what that ritual was. No matter how hard Zarifah tried to convince Her that she could be trusted with the knowledge of the ritual, Her wouldn't tell. *I don't see why she won't trust me.*

Sweat slid down her back. The air cons worked sporadically. The dancers continued despite the suffocating heat in the room. Etana moved gracefully thought the arm positions. *Thank Her Etana has potential.*

'Let's try some lifts before finishing up for the day.' Zarifah clapped her hands to get everyone's attention. The dancers paired up. Zarifah fanned herself with her hands, desperate for some air.

A scream echoed in the room. Zarifah turned to see Hayal on the floor rubbing her ankle.

'Sorry,' said Jarah. His face flushed red from the heat and the practice session.

'Idiot,' grumbled Hayal.

Zarifah inspected Hayal's ankle. 'Get some ice on it and it should be all right.'

Jarah went to help Hayal but she pushed him away. 'You've done enough.'

The heat's too much. Zarifah needed to relieve the tension between the dancers. The inspection had left them all on edge. *I'll tell them about Her.* It was risky, but she needed to ensure the dancers knew the facts of their past, the true lives that the Soul Dancers lived so that they would choose Her's side when the rebellion started.

'Break for five, be back with costumes to work on,' she yelled. Emptiness grew inside of her. She longed for the taste of happiness. *It will help me get through this crap.* More so than any of the pick-me-up pills.

Jarah brought her a drink; the tasteless water had been purified over and over again by the machines. Rarely did it ever rain above and if it did the water was polluted and took many chemical treatments before it was drinkable.

'Change the music to something with the flutes,' instructed Zarifah to the boy. He was trying hard to make amends, but her heart didn't soften with his actions. Too much had happened in the last day or so, the arrival of Etana, dead alien, random inspection from the Regulators. Plus there was the dance with Torin, which she couldn't get out of her mind. Zarifah wanted to dance with him again, to have their own private session upstairs. A wave of heat pulsed through her body as the fantasy playing out in her mind. She gave herself a moment to indulge before pushing the image away.

Zarifah grabbed a large cushion and sat cross-legged on the floor. Etana settled next to her. Zarifah feared for the girl. She'd not spoken much since the separation. Here in the House you didn't need to speak, just be able, even if not willing, to use your body. 'Listen Etana,' Zarifah whispered in her ear. 'This is the only hope you'll have to cling to down here.'

Dancers returned with costumes, needles or pliers and sat on cushions around Zarifah. 'Her, all knowing, understood the death-life cycle better than all and she rose to power before the war.

'Generations past were cruel to the world, to themselves, and the Earth rumbled out her poisons only for them to be collected like vomit on her surface and in the air like a blanket of soot.' The dancers listened, their fingers automatically fixing and designing, their minds absorbing.

'Humans hadn't settled the stars, like now, and they were out of control, their emotions making it difficult to complete their labours. Her and the other goddesses, Elanora, Prentera, Thraident, spoke to the Earth and discovered what was needed to heal her. Instead of suppressing emotions they were to develop dance stories to help people understand what was behind the energy so that they could walk a peaceful life and develop harmony with the Earth, healing the damage from past generations. But not everyone listened. Those who were deep in their darkness, those who suffered, didn't believe and they paid Alchemists to develop a cure, a cocktail of chemicals to be injected into those who lacked the will to live. The Emotionless were born—it took time and many generations. The chemicals were strong; mutations caused the emotions to be suppressed. Some realised instead of cloning they could breed the Emotionless. The Emotionless were the breathing robots of the future who completed jobs, didn't care about the natural cycle of life. Their emotions never clouded their judgement. Their decisions were valued above others. The Earth died a little more each day another Emotionless was born. Without realising, they welcomed the change and accepted the genetic manipulation and the Earth began to rumble with anger in an attempt to wake up her guests. But they didn't awaken.

'To ensure their survival, they looked out to the stars and found other species and other worlds to live in. The Emotionless wanted to rule. They believed that they were the superior for they didn't feel and therefore had sound judgement. Fighting without emotion and killing without emotion, their numbers grew and they became the Regulators of the Earth. More turned to the faith of Her, but she could no longer keep breathing in the pollution on the Earth. She felt the pain of the Earth and she passed to the next world. Before leaving, she trained her priestesses how to reach her in the Astral plane, a place where we no longer required a body, and she hoped that we would follow Her's teachings and continue the war against the Regulators and help the Earth heal once more. We were always meant to live in harmony on the surface of this planet and have joy and peace and abundance.'

As Zarifah finished, the Earth, as if she had been listening, grumbled, bringing the dancers back to reality. Mini earthquakes sent frequent reminders of the Earth's pain.

'We are closer to winning the war. Her would never want us to give up hope. We must always be here for each other, for there are too many against us, those with imprisoned souls carry the future around our necks. It is up to us to fight, so we can teach others freely of the ways of Her. When we have finally purged ourselves and the Earth, then we can welcome a time of harvest and celebration.'

'It is not too late.' She looked at them individually trying to instil hope. Etana listened, eyes wide. *There is our hope right there. If only I can stop her from having to complete a harvest.*

'What's this?' yelled Nigil as he entered the room. Zarifah quickly stood and defended her dancers.

'The inspection left many costumes damaged, they had to spend time mending.'

'I want a harvest tonight that makes up for missing last night,' said Nigil. 'Get ready now!' A thunderous glare caused the dancers to quickly pick up their costumes and leave.

'You just don't listen,' said Nigil. His anger rippled around her in waves of prickly heat.

Zarifah stood defiant. 'After the mishap with the alien, *you* should listen.'

'You will get a whipping.' Nigil's veins stood out on his neck as he glared at her.

'But what would you rather me do, harvest or beg. I help you to bring in more emotions than any other dancer here.'

Nigil grabbed her arm and squeezed tight cutting off the blood supply. He pulled her in tight. She could smell his stale breath. 'I'm in charge.'

'Of course.' She lowered her eyes and touched his chest.

He brushed her away. 'This isn't over.' He strode away. His words leaving a deathly chill.

***

The harvest was poor that night and Nigil stomped around the next day ordering the dancers to the practice room for the day. Air con units were still not working and Torin bore the results of asking for them to be fixed; a swollen eye and split lip.

Zarifah organised a bed for Etana with the other female younglings. She couldn't afford to have the girl with her, not with the risks she was planning to take. She rested back into her bed. Urgent banging on her door stopped Zarifah from slipping off to sleep. *What now?* Grabbing her robe to cover her body, she opened the door.

Torin stood in the doorway. Zarifah's breath caught in her throat. *No I can't.* Instead she stepped closer to him, her heart pounded out a rhythm she longed to lose herself in with him.

She looked up at him. His swollen eye caused tightness in her chest. Torin lowered his head and brushed his lips on hers. 'I couldn't sleep.'

A bolt of desire shuddered down her body as she looked into his blue eyes.

'What's going on here?' yelled a voice down the corridor.

Zarifah jerked away as Nigil came towards them. 'Nothing.' She swallowed hard. She didn't want Torin to be dealt with anymore punishment.

'Didn't look like nothing.'

Fuck. Her mind went blank.

'Just talking dance routines,' said Torin.

'Like hell.' Nigil motioned for them to follow him. 'My office.' Nigil walked with a stiff back.

Her, help me. Zarifah looked at Torin questioningly but he wouldn't meet her glance. Dread filled her body with each step closer to Nigil's office. There was only one thing on Nigil's mind and it cut at Zarifah's stomach. He knows how to get under our skin. It would be a beating at best. There was one other thing that Zarifah now feared.

Torin closed the door as Nigil poured three shots of liquor. *So it's that then.* Zarifah concentrated on keeping her breathing steady. The whip wasn't coming out which mean they had to please him. This was punishment enough. *I'd have preferred the whip.*

The room was simple, a single plain wooden desk with an old style computer, screwed to the table. A large black executive type chair—one that swivelled and was cushioned, from an age long gone. The door at the back of the room, to the left, stood locked, hiding secrets that Nigil controlled. A reminder to Zarifah that she needed to get on with the plan with Her.

Torin automatically moved behind the desk, towards Nigil. He glared at Zarifah to follow suit, they were here to give pleasure. *No.* Zarifah didn't want to move. She saw sadness in Torin's eyes. But he still did what was asked of him. Not now she knew there was something between her and Torin. She stood frozen watching Torin begin to massage his hands on Nigil's shoulders. *Stop it.* A sour taste filled her mouth. *It's the only way to be with Torin.* She hated it. *It's just a game.* But the thought didn't help alleviate what she had to do in front of Torin with Nigil. There was no pleasure between them, only for Nigil. *Best get this over with before Nigil knows for sure that I like Torin.*

Zarifah walked hesitantly towards Nigil. She straddled him and pushed her hips into his. She looked at the wolf pin instead of Torin. The bitterness intensified in her mouth as she worked her body against Nigil's, grinding against his groin, he hardened quickly, and leant back enjoying the session. *This will be the last time.*

Torin reached down his chest, leaning forward to kiss Nigil. Zarifah closed her eyes not wanting to see Torin's lips on another. This was about keeping Nigil satisfied so she could live and have the chance to bring back Her, and free the other dancers. She had to play her part. *Nigil already suspects too much.* And that made Zarifah fearful of what Nigil might do. She ran her hands under Nigil's shirt, pushing the material away, gliding her fingers on his skin until it prickled. She moved to take off Nigil's shirt, Torin helped her, his fingers brushed against hers. She held her breath as a burning heat lingered on her skin from his touch. *I want more.* She looked into his eyes and saw the same passion burning. But not here. Not right in front of Nigil. Torin folded up the shirt and wrapped it around Nigil's eyes. Nigil went to pull the material away.

'It will be more pleasurable,' whispered Torin flicking his tongue on the outside of Nigil's ear. Nigil's body shuddered and he surrendered to the suggestion. Without Nigil seeing made it easier. Torin brushed his fingers along her shoulder. *He will notice.* The warning shivered in her mind but she didn't pull away. It was bad enough having to do this with Torin, of all the dancers, but the urge to touch Torin was beginning to overpower her and it took all her resolve to hold back. *It's only because of the kiss.* She'd done this before with Nigil. Never with Torin. *Why couldn't it stay like that?* Her own body shivered as Torin brushed over her breast. An ache flared inside of her. *No good will come of this.* But then Torin's lips pressed on hers and she no longer cared. She found herself unravelling with the movement of his circling tongue with hers. Then Nigil stiffened between her legs and she pulled away from Torin, remembering why she was here, began kissing along Nigil's chest upwards to his neck, while unbuckling his belt. *He will know. Then he will kill him. I have to focus.* She unbuttoned Nigil's trousers. There's no room for Torin here. She looked at Torin apologetically. He mouthed the word *later*. That single word set her thighs aching. A promise that she was sure to make him keep. That's all she thought about as she worked on giving pleasure to Nigil. Kissing him on his lips, she moved aside to allow Torin to move in closer. Zarifah sucked on Nigil's lips playfully. *It's just another client.* Still the repulsion rippled through her as Torin's mouth worked on Nigil's cock. Nigil groaned softly.

Zarifah couldn't wait to get this over with. Nigil reached up and pulled at her costume. She had to stop herself from moving away. *It's for the survival of the faith.* Threads broke as he pulled away the material bound around her breasts. His hand cupped her, pinching her nipple hard until she gasped sharply. She closed her eyes trying to forget that Torin was here. But he reminded her by slipping his hand up her leg. She trembled. It was the best response for she knew Nigil would take the credit. Nigil clamped his mouth on her other breast. Torin's hand glided further up her leg, slowly. She moaned. One hand she put on Nigil's shoulder to steady herself, the other she ran down Torin's back. His skin prickled beneath her fingers. It was a dangerous game. She loved it. Torin's fingers slipped to the inside of her thigh. *Nearly there. Just a little higher…*

Nigil misread her response. He pulled away. 'Torin you can go.'

His fingers slipped away as Torin stood to leave. Her skin tingled where he'd been touching her. She closed her eyes not trusting herself to conceal the feelings towards Torin. When the door clicked closed she opened them and met Nigil's grey stare.

'Where was I?' He nuzzled her breast. Zarifah steeled herself not to pull away.

She looked over and saw the door that led to the restricted rooms where souls were split and Alchemists processed the harvest. She had a sudden desire to go and investigate. But then she shuddered with the memories of the room, the first experience she had of this place.

Nigil groaned as he pulled Zarifah close. *This could be my chance.* She made it her focus to help her to get through this session with Nigil. She bit her teeth playfully into the side of his neck. She worked hard on him, using every part of her body, begging him to surrender to her touch. But when she danced her fingers over his skin, through his hair, she longed for the touch of Torin, the tenderness and intimacy that she had never known. Nigil had his eyes closed with pleasure but there wasn't even the tiniest smell of spiciness. *And all Torin did was kiss me.*

Zarifah forced him towards his peak, building the tension between them until there was too much and it burst with Nigil groaning and convulsing, clutching to her body. Nigil pushed her away and he settled back into the chair. She poured him a shot of liquor. He drank it with one gulp. Then another. Zarifah waited patiently, hoping she had exhausted him enough. She poured another shot.

'You keep getting better.' He lifted the full glass to her in a false toast then drank.   'Isn't that why you have me here?'

He laughed and held out his glass. Zarifah waited patiently for Nigil to slip into an alcohol-induced sleep.

Zarifah tied her belt and covered her body as best she could with the material from her outfit. Her heart pulsed erratically. Fingers trembling, she took the wolf pin from Nigil's pocket and thanked the man for being so tight with money that he hadn't maintained the security system of finger or eye scans. Barefoot she moved to the door, only once before had she been in this room and now she hesitated. Nigil's breathing kept her motivated and she swiped the pin. The door clicked and slid open.

Rows and rows of crystals were organised on the far shelves. Around her neck, her crystal pulsed with the longing of her trapped soul. Moving into the dimly lit room, she kept away from the oversized chair in the middle, one that had leather straps hanging over the edges like dead arms. The electronics connected to the chair flashed a green light as if it was asleep but able to wake up in an instant. A length of moveable coil looped around a chair and ended in an open point. Her soul remembered and screamed for her to leave.

Not knowing what to look for she inspected the crystals. They were cold and felt like ordinary rocks without any living essence or emotion entrapped within.

Crystals containing emotion were lined on the bench ready to be emptied. She lifted each one to her nose like a flower and smelled. Grief, anger and curiosity. Each tingled under her touch. She held her breath hoping that there would be a hint of spiciness.

Next to these crystals was an oven, where an empty mould

sat in the middle. She looked carefully, trying to see if she would be able to use a machine like this, to see if maybe she could use it to reverse the process. *Would the soul know how to re-join itself? Could it heal itself? Join with the soul once more and be whole?*

'Oi!' A male voice made her turn sharply. A man dressed poorly in a white stained coat holding a hot drink stood nervously in front of a door on the far right of the room. 'What do you want?'

Zarifah walked towards the man. He was slightly overweight and his skin, while a little brown, was white from being here underground in the House. Nigil kept the Alchemists hidden, under lock and key. They only left if they died, or were killed. She didn't know much about the Alchemists, other than they broke the teachings of Her by splitting the soul.

Zarifah smiled as she stood in front of the man. His hand trembled slightly. 'Would you show me how you remove the emotion from the crystal?'

'You shouldn't be down here.' He went to the bench.

'I have always wondered what you do down here.' She brushed against him and he pulled away.

'You should go.' His voice sounded uncertain. A crystal around his neck, a star shape made from a clear quartz, held part of his soul.

'Please, I won't tell.' She moved closer and placed her hand on his cheek. 'I can do so much more for you.' He looked down at her chest. She suggestively pushed the material aside to reveal her breast.

'The quicker you show me, the more I can do for you,' she whispered in his ear, ignoring his sweaty odour.

'And how do I know that you haven't been sent here? In disguise, The Collector, he does things.' He struggled to speak as she looked at him longingly.

'He's asleep.' She held up the crystal. 'But not for much longer.'

The man smiled and placed the crystal in the centre of the machine and pushed two electrodes into its surface. Closing the door, he stood back a little and pushed a button. In a glass tube next to the machine ran a smoky grey colour while the centre of the machine lit up and hummed.

He pointed to another button. 'These machines are mostly automated, costly for The Collector, but ensures that emotions remain pure, not contaminated with each other, and can be transported in other crystals if need be.'

'And the crystal is ready to be used again?'

'Once it's cleaned.' He took the crystal out, nearly dropping it as he bumped into Zarifah and her cloak gaped and he stared for a moment before placing the crystal into a small container. He closed the plastic lid and buzzed the button. He explained that the crystal rattled around for a few seconds as magnetic pulses cleaned its matrix.

'Done.' He handed her the crystal, which really just looked the same. She smelled it—odourless.

'You're a dancer?' he asked.

'The best.' She took his hand in hers. 'We could work together, help each other.' She placed his hand onto her breast. 'Will you show me how things work here and I'll, well...' She pushed his hand hard into her breast. He squeezed.

'It's too risky...'

She let go and looked at his empty eyes, hungry starved eyes. She knew that look. 'What's your name?'

'Oren.'

'Oren,' she drew out his name seductively. His breath quickened. She kissed him, suppressing a cringe of disgust. *Torin forgive me.* She knew Torin loved Her as much as she did. *He'll forgive me when he learns of the plan to restore Her's power back on Earth.*

She pulled back to see if the Alchemist had submitted. He nodded and kissed her bare skin around her neck. Zarifah stroked him quickly towards release. There was only so far she could push things and while she hadn't been down here long, she had to return the pin before The Collector woke. As his panting subsided, she re-tied her cloak and slipped the cleaned crystal in her belt.

'Can you replicate this?' She held up the metal pin she'd taken from Nigil.

'Yes.' He tried to snatch it from her.

'Show me. I'll do it.' She wasn't about to let anyone have something so valuable. *The pin will help me take over the House and then I can protect the dancers and free them.*

He paused but then obliged. Copying the data from the pin was easy. She now had her own copy of the codes to the House on a chip. She made sure she wiped the data from the memory so the Alchemist wouldn't get any ideas of trying to make one himself.

'Your life will be sweeter down here than on the surface. Anyway, where would you go?' she said.

'Nowhere, there's nowhere up on the surface. Only other Houses.'

'Are you able to reverse the separation of the soul?' she asked

'No.'

'Can you experiment?'

'It won't be easy.' But already he was squinting and biting his cheek in thought.

'I'll visit you for inspiration.' Zarifah smiled at him and cheekily kissed him before leaving. 'Tell no one,' she reminded.

'Of course.'

She quietly slipped back into Nigil's room. His snores were comforting. She put back the pin on his shirt and looked up to see him watching her. She froze.

'I always knew not to trust you.' He stood and grabbed her by the hair. 'This time you get a whipping for trying to steal money.'

He took out his whip. *He hasn't realised what I really stole.* The whip came down on her bare back cutting her flesh. And then she fought the pain that spread further with each lashing.

Her, we are so close, help me, help me. Even then she doubted the goddess heard or even cared as the lashings continued and she felt alone and forgotten.

10

Etana shook Zarifah's bare arms forcing the woman back to consciousness. Her gaze focussed on the Etana. The girl frowned with concern.

Rising from the bed, Zarifah tried to walk over to her costumes. She had to get ready to dance tonight. Etana had cleaned her room, and the costumes were put away in the closet.

Zarifah allowed Etana to sponge down her body and once again clean the cuts on her back. She gritted her teeth against the stabbing pain that shot through her body when Etana touched her back. Each movement was caused the cuts to bleed again. A sharp eucalyptus smell filled the room as Etana taped dressings soaked in antiseptic over her wounds. The liquid cooled her burning skin as her body fought against infection.

Etana helped Zarifah to twist a black velvet-like material around her chest, neck, and shoulders away from the wounds. Nigil had made sure they covered most of her back. A thick black belt was tied tightly over black tights, which flared out around her ankles. She showed the girl how to knot lengths of metal chains and plastic to hang from her belt and wrap around her arms. She couldn't bear to try and do her hair and Etana didn't have the skills. Between them, with Etana constantly having to wipe red ooze from her back, they managed to tie her dark hair up in a bun with bits of short chain hanging from the sides. Zarifah couldn't stand the pain if anything touched her back.

Three gentle knocks on the door caused Etana to jump up. Zarifah held her breath. *Please not Nigil.* She wanted the pills to take away the pain. *Or the taste of happiness.* She ran her tongue over her lips remembering the hint of spiciness of the emotion she harvested.

Torin walked in. Zarifah's pulse thundered as she saw him. A mix of emotions flooded her body, guilt at what she had done with Nigil and the Alchemist, and desire as Torin's tight clothing tempted her imagination of what he would look like without this clothes. She remembered his promise. Heat flushed on her cheeks.

'Etana, you have done a great job at dressing the Soul Dancer.' Torin passed her a nutrient tablet which she swallowed quickly and even managed a weak smile.

'Has she been a good patient for you?' he asked. Etana nodded. 'Good, otherwise I'd have to tell her off and that wouldn't be pretty.' He winked at the girl who stood proudly by his side.

'You really think that you can dance tonight?' he asked.

'No.' Zarifah took a deep breath against the pain. 'But what choice do I have?'

'You sure pissed off Nigil.' He banged the air con a few times and turned the controls until cooler air filtered out. She glimpsed the barbed wire knots on his tattoo around his toned waistline.

He moved gracefully around her room. His broad shoulders inviting to rest her head on, and she longed to taste his lips on hers once more. She wanted him to act on his promise, to finish what they had started. *No I can't.*

'Are you going to tell me what you've done to deserve this?' He raised his eyebrow questioningly. But there was another expression on his face. Her body tensed. *He's found the chip and empty crystal.* 'Did you hide the…'

'Yes. I want to know what's going on.'

Zarifah's stomach fluttered with nerves. *Will he like the plan?* She looked deep into his eyes. *Will he support me?* She wasn't ready to let him in on what Her had planned, but she didn't have much of a choice. 'I hope to reverse the soul splitting process.' She leant close to Torin. 'The chip will allow access to the Alchemists so I can experiment.'

His eyes widened with surprise. 'That's crazy.'

'It's what Her wants.' She rested her hand on his arm. 'Go meditate and speak with Her if you don't believe me.'

'You're going to get killed.'

Zarifah heard the anxiety in his voice. 'I won't.' She squeezed her hand on his arm. 'Where are the items?'

'Safe.' He stepped away brushing off her grip.

'You will give them back to me.' Tightness formed around her chest. To lose the chip now would be a disaster, especially after all that Zarifah had risked.

'Depends.' He turned to Etana who was listening to every word. 'You need to go back to your room,' said Torin.

'See you tomorrow,' said Etana as she gave him a friendly hug.

Zarifah was surprised to hear Etana speak. 'You've done well with Etana,' she said when the girl had left.

Torin helped Zarifah up. 'She deserves better than this life down here.'

Zarifah tried to push the pain away as she walked and held back asking whether or not he had pills. There was so much more she wanted to say to him. *Sorry.* But then they weren't allowed to be together so she wasn't sure that sorry was the right thing to say. They had come so close with Nigil in the room Zarifah feared it would only be a matter of time before they couldn't resist each other any longer.

Side stage the dancers were readying themselves for the harvest. Torin had done a good job organising them during the day with Hayal's help.

'My, what a gorgeous looking back,' said Nigil as he approached the dancers from his office. His voice opened the wounds once more. 'I'll be expecting a great harvest from you Zarifah. I want you to also dance on the stage for the first two dancers, a teaser for the audience.' He smiled and left to take his seat in the front row.

'You got those pills?' Zarifah asked Torin desperately.

'No and I wouldn't give you one if I had.' Despite his words his eyes reflected sympathy.

'Ladies and Gentleman,' The Presenter began the introduction.

Zarifah walked on stage with two less experienced dancers, two women who were just starting to develop their skill now they had been dancing for a year. It took a long time to perfect the harvest even if you did have some skill. Then there were those who didn't have the stomach for taking the emotions, for it was an abomination, and they ended up losing their mind.

Not able to see or even force herself to smell since her mind was so occupied trying to ignore the pain, she kept her arms low alongside her body and used her hips more than usual and kept her back to the audience. She couldn't even hear the drums, but kept her body moving which made it difficult for the blood to dry. Somehow she endured.

'Here,' said Hayal when the dance ended and Zarifah stepped from the stage, immediately collapsing on the ground in pain, trying to dig her fingernails into the concrete floor. She nearly screamed as Hayal began to wipe down her back.

Zarifah gasped against the pain.

'Zarifah how are you going to harvest?' asked Hayal.

'I'm counting on you and the others to bring in lots of little emotions, so that if I don't harvest something big then at least Nigil will have some money,' she answered.

'That won't work.'

'I know. Don't worry, I can pull the moves out of my body when I need, let's just pray there's something out there for me that's actually worth harvesting. The House hasn't been this quiet for days now.' Zarifah gritted her teeth together.

Zarifah walked out on the stage and managed to complete the final dance for the evening, including harvesting anger.

'Half a flower,' said Nigil, and entered the data on her chip. She wouldn't go to the Ink Master until she had at least a full flower. *That could be a while.* Zarifah knew that he wouldn't want her to finish the tattoo belt. Not that it would matter much. *I would have to stay here.* There was nowhere else to go. But she hoped that with a finished belt there would be more benefits for her. *I'll look after the dancers when I'm in charge.* The promise helped her to hold Nigil's dark stare.

'Out.' Zarifah didn't need to be told twice. Relieved she didn't have to perform or defend herself she rushed out.

In her room Zarifah lay on her stomach on her bed. *Her take the pain away.* Her back felt numb from the wounds that had cracked and reopened during the performance. She closed her eyes tight trying to slip into a meditative state, but the agony kept her awareness in her body.

The door slid open. Zarifah looked up to see Torin slipping into her room.

'You harvest well?' she asked.

Torin shrugged. He had a new barbed wire on his tattoo.

He sat next to her on the bed, ducking his head below the alcove.

'Here.' He opened his hand to reveal the crystal and chip. 'Tell me about the chip.'

'It gets me into where the harvests are processed. And

anywhere else Nigil's wolf pin will let him in. The Alchemist, Oren, is going to experiment to find ways to reverse the process, to re-join the souls. And this is an empty crystal, just for me to do with as I please.' She spoke in hushed tones. *To fill it with happiness and drink it myself.*

'Her will be pleased.' He handed her the items. 'I am becoming fond of you.' His fingers lingered on hers as she took the chip and crystal. She pulled her hand away. *I can't risk his life.* And there was the plan of rebelling to free the dancers. *That's more important than Torin and me.*

'This is the first time I've made any sort of progress for years. Torin I'm close, soon Nigil will be gone and I'll be in charge. With your help we can stop the misuse of the dancers, and teach about Her. Wouldn't that be great.' He smiled, but his eyes didn't look happy.

'Don't get ahead of yourself. We have a lot of work to do. I suggest you concentrate on resting so your body can heal.' He kissed her on the lips, long and soft. His heat transferred to her and spiked her desire for him further. Then all too soon he pulled away. 'Rest up.'

Tariq left the room, leaving Zarifah wishing he would come back, curl up in her bed and hold her for tonight. But of course she couldn't stop at only that. She wanted all of him. *When I'm in charge.* She carefully placed the items in the sealed compartment under her mattress and relaxed into the blackness of sleep.

11

Zarifah continued dancing during the following week, which made the healing of her skin slow. She had taken to teaching Etana more of Her's teachings and how life functioned down here below the surface in the House of Nigil.

Today was washing day, where they could go and shower, part of a small luxury to keep clients happy and diseases at bay. Without her back healed completely she didn't want to risk softening the scabs, but went to the lower levels where the showers were to listen to the gossip.

Zarifah settled on the metal bench re-plaiting her own hair. Hayal dried Etana's wet hair with a towel.

'How about I style your hair into a hundred little plaits?' asked Hayal. She ran her fingers thought Etana's hair. The dancer had developed a cough and her lungs rattled as she breathed. Some of the other dancers were coughing too. *We need to get a Medic in.*

The Ink Master came up to them with a bag and took out a needle. 'How are we today?' He tried to sound happy but it didn't fool Zarifah.

'Time for medicine,' said Zarifah. She finished tying the last of the long single plait and motioned for Etana to come forward. She pushed her sleeve up to expose her slender but toned arm.

The Ink Master gave the Zarifah three jabs in the arm, one to make sure the women stayed sterile, one for vitamins, and another against the diseases from the line of work in the upstairs rooms. Nigil, despite his fear of spending money did go to stringent lengths to ensure that his dancers were clean and diseases were managed. After all he wanted patrons to come back, and this certainly helped.

'She only needs one needle, for vitamins,' said Zarifah to the tattooist. Her arm pulsed after the injections.

'Zarifah, you know the rules,' he said with his head leaning to one side. 'Don't make this difficult, not after all that's gone down recently.'

'Maybe you should have your back seen to,' he said as he injected Hayal.

'It's healing well,' she answered. *He's right.* It was taking too long to heal. She hadn't managed to harvest enough for Nigil to even pay her half a flower.

Hayal coughed as she finished Etana's hair.

'Have you taken the syrup?' asked Zarifah.

The girl nodded as the coughing subsided.

'And?'

'Not much improvement,' answered Hayal.

The House hadn't had an outbreak of the lung destroying disease for years. It would be bad for business.

'You coughed blood?'

Hayal shook her head.

'Keep taking the syrup. I'll speak to Nigil about getting the Medic,' said Zarifah. She'd managed to avoid spending any private time with The Collector for the last week and hated the idea of having to make such a request. *He'll still be sore about me and Torin.* And Zarifah couldn't help think that Nigil would want to punish her even more. *Just to prove a point.*

'In the meantime, go and rest this afternoon. Make sure you do, you don't want this cough to get worse,' instructed Zarifah.

'But what will Nigil say, and the others?' said Hayal, wrapping her cloak around her slender body.

'Those with coughs will be resting too,' said Zarifah firmly. 'So go and take some time out.' She playfully pushed Hayal away. 'Rest.'

Zarifah left Etana in the care of Dahra, she sought out Nigil, her back more moist with each step she took closer to his office.

A Sentinel stood outside blocking the door.

'Can't enter,' he said.

'But I need to.'

He pointed to the benches where the dancers would sometimes sit as they waited for their nightly payments. *He must have someone important with him.* She walked over silently and sat and waited, keeping her back away from the wall.

Zarifah crossed her legs and bounced her foot impatiently. *Has Oren found a way to re-join the souls?* She was waiting for things to further settle down in the House before sneaking into see the Alchemist. If she got caught, another whipping would be difficult to endure.

Over an hour later and the longer she waited, the more curious she became about who was going to walk out of the room. Mentally she had gone through all the dancers she'd seen at the showers this morning, and there wasn't anyone who she couldn't account for. She hoped Oren wasn't spilling the beans, or that there would be a mess in the room because a client had tried to double-cross Nigil.

She was about to leave when the door clicked open. A man wearing the signal of a Dark Angel stood shaking Nigil's hand.

'Sentinel, escort Flann out to the ship.' Nigil wore his business face, cold, blank and calculating. He looked down on her. 'I assume you are here to see me?' He waved his hand to move her into his office. 'Sit.'

'I need a Medic, the cuts may be infected.' She remained standing in front of his desk.

Nigil lifted his black eyebrows in disbelief.

'At least get a Medic in so I can have the cream that will speed up the healing. You want me to perform better don't you?'

Nigil sat silently in his chair, fingers poised on his cheek.

I have to convince him. Her mind scrambled for the words. 'Some of the dancers are coughing and the syrup's not helping. It would be wise to bring the Medic in for that. You don't want an outbreak here.'

Nigil made a disapproving sound. Each time a Medic came to a House it had to go on the records and was never good for business and was another thing for the Regulators to use against a House.

Zarifah sat suggestively on his desk. 'It will be worth it.' She leaned forward to give him full view of her cleavage.

'It will cost you. All of you.' He sat up in his chair and leaned forward. His aniseed breath caused a coldness to seep into her body.

'Of course.' She slid her finger down the side of his clean-shaven face.

'All of you.'

The look in his eye caused her to pause. *The price will be too much.*

'No tattoos from tonight's harvest.' His grey eyes chilled her further.

'That's too much.' Zarifah pulled away.

'Then tell me who is sick and we can send them outside and see how long they last.'

Her options were limited. He knew it. *It's not worth arguing over this one.* 'Fine then. No tattoos for one harvest.' *The dancers aren't going to like this.*

He punched on the holographic screen. 'Tell those with coughs and any other ailments to get themselves down here first thing tomorrow.'

Zarifah waited to be dismissed. *The silence grated on her. He better not want me to pleasure him.* The longer she waited, the more she was convinced that was what he wanted.

'Have you met Flann before?' he said leaning back in his chair.

'No.'

'Not known to you at all?' His eyes narrowed as if he doubted her answer.

'I saw the angel signal,' she answered calmly, her mind scrambling to think of what this could be about.

'The Collector there, Kade has heard of you.' Nigil put his fingers together in front of his chest and stared at her coolly.

'Everyone has. The patrons talk, you know that,' she answered, her blood racing faster. *Her help me, has Oren spoken? Or someone else?*

'Kade wants to hire you for a night and is willing to pay a very large amount of money. He sent his man over to negotiate.'

'What?' Her back stiffened. *He can't sell me like this.* Things weren't the best in this House, but it was what she knew. If she went to another House things could go wrong. She swallowed hard. *I could be killed.*

'So much money, that after the inspection with the Regulators, we will be back on track.'

'And you can then afford a luxury like the medic,' Zarifah said. *Would he really lend her to another House for a price? It's too risky.* It would also delay her chances of finding a way to re-join the split soul.

'I've said yes.'

'What?'

'Sentinel Mosan will accompany you, and you will perform one harvest for the night.'

'Kade can't guarantee I will be safe,' said Zarifah, panic rising with the taste of acid in her throat. 'You can't guarantee that he or a patron wouldn't want more.'

'No, I can't, but that's why the price is high.'

'You're willing to share me?'

'No, but if there's an offer or you do sleep with one of their patrons, I'm sure you'd convince them to come over here. There's also an additional fee for your bodily services other than dancing, to be confirmed after the night, depending if there is anyone suitable.'

'I choose then?' Her mouth had dried and the words were hard to form.

'No. If you do this then you'll get ten flowers.' Zarifah nearly choked. Ten flowers was more than she would earn in a year. Since Senara hadn't come back, and harvests had been poor, her belt wasn't progressing.

'I don't…' she began softly, trying to summon the courage to say no. But then she could feel Her, and the goddess would want her to go. Ten more flowers would bring her closer to finishing her belt. *Then I can do Her's work with more freedom because I won't be a slave.*

'You'll go when your back is healed, another week, especially with the nano-cream from the Medic to speed up the healing.'

The pieces began to fit together and she eyed Nigil.

Cunning bastard. He probably was always going to bring in a medic.

'Disease? Coughing? What about my safety? I can't perform if Sentinel Mosan is in the room.' Her argument sounded weak. Nigil had obviously thought about this.

'Kade has signed a legal document. All above board, even one for the authorities to accept and tick in the not-breaking-the-law box.'

Zarifah frowned as she fingered the crystal around her neck. *There was always a price. Ten flowers would be worth it.* If she stayed safe that is, as long as she returned.

'And if I don't return?'

'His House is mine.' She forced herself to swallow and hold Nigil's gaze. 'But you'll be back because he wouldn't risk losing his House. Go. I've got work to do.' He waved her out of his office, turning to his computer as she left.

Mixed feelings tumbled inside of her. *Ten flowers. I have to make the best of this. For the sake of Her and the other dancers.*

12

Zarifah clipped together the back of the tight fitting plastic-like material around her breasts making them lift and appear bigger. She dressed in her favourite outfit for the night; black and transparent wings extended from between her shoulders. They helped to hide the fresh scars. The wounds had healed quickly with the nano-cream from the Medic.

'You feel better then?' asked Torin as he sat awkwardly on her bed, his head bent forward so it didn't hit the top of the alcove.

'Yes,' she answered. It doesn't matter if I am or not. Nigil had decided she was well and had made the arrangements for her to dance tonight at the Angel House. *It will be worth the ten flowers.* She wove small chains of metal under the material around her chest so there was a series of loops. Her belt, made from the same material around her chest, was tied tightly, holding a front and back panel of transparent material, soft and black. Fine chains of different sizes and metals hung from her belt. Her white skin looked even whiter against the black material.

'So have you any plans yet?' he asked.

'No,' she lied. The empty crystal hung at her waist hidden in material and chains ready to be filled. *If I get the chance.* Nerves fluttered though her body.

Zarifah added some pieces of diamond shaped metal with tassels of chains to her belt. Such jewellery had taken her hours of careful tapping into shape and joining the chains.

'Zarifah, I want you to return.' He rested his hands around her waist from behind her and hugged her body to his. 'I don't want you to take any additional risks, not even for the sake of Her.'

'I can't believe you would say that.' She tried to pull away but he held her firm.

'Her wouldn't want you dead. If you are dead then you can't do her bidding. So what I am saying is to keep safe.' He kissed the top of her shoulder. She relaxed into his embrace.

'I've been meditating and Her wants me to support you,' he said between kisses, his hands caressing her bare belly, her stomach muscles taut from hours of dancing.

'Promise me that you'll take care of yourself and that you'll not do anything that would endanger your life.'

'Too late.' She leant back into his body. His strength pulsed around her. *If only…*

'Yeah, but you have a knack of making things worse for yourself.' He kissed the top of her fresh scars, moving the wings out of the way.

'Her must be restored.' Zarifah too had been meditating. Her was getting impatient.

'You must return to me.' He released her and turned her to face him. 'Zarifah, promise.' His hands stopped her from moving away.

'Torin, I will not promise.' She stood firm. Her body and soul wanted to fall back into his arms and agree. But there was a strong voice in her head telling her that she had made a bigger promise to the goddess, Her. A pledge she would die to keep; a promise that Torin was meant to be helping her keep.

'I'll do what I need to. I will not deliberately place myself at risk or do anything that would result in harm to the other dancers.' She kissed him. Soft and sweet, his lips moved with hers, flowing like the material from her waist. 'I do want to return to you,' she said as she pulled away. She yearned to stay in his arms. Zarifah inhaled deeply to fill her lungs with the smell of cinnamon. She wanted to taste more. *Not now.* Her logic began to blur as the spicy smell intensified. Not when Nigil would punish them if he found out. *Maybe Nigil won't find out.* Her eyes linked with Torin's. Her body flushed with heat, wanting more. Torin ran his hands down her bare arms setting them tingling. *I don't care.* Zarifah sighed. Pressed her lips on his again. A bolt of pleasure shuddered through her body and she made content noises as her tongue played with his. His heat embraced her in a vibration of passion.

There was a bang on the door. Zarifah pulled away sharply, her mind re-focussed.

'Ya ready, Zarifah?'

'I'll expect a report of the evening, take care of Hayal,' said Zarifah.

Torin grabbed her and kissed her once more. Her knees weakened and her body begged to surrender, to let him hold her weight. *Just once.* The spiciness concentrated around them. He held her tightly into his body.

'And I expect you to return.' Torin released her. But his hands lingered on her hips. His touch sent a wave of lust to her head. Her mind swirled with mixed feelings. *I don't want to go.*

'May Her be with you.' Torin tilted his forehead to hers.

The banging started on the door again. 'Zarifah.' She jumped. Her thoughts settled. *This can't happen. Not ever.* She stepped away from Torin and opened the door.

'About time, hurry up,' said Sentinel Mosan. He pushed Zarifah in front of him.

They walked along the corridor to the highest level where a shuttle waited to take Zarifah to the Angel House.

Nigil stood by the hatch, pacing back and forth in the small corridor. A few electric lights fluttered high in the wall casting more shadow than light.

'Here's to a good harvest,' said Nigil as he took a swig from his hip flask, fumbling it back in place under his suit jacket. She ducked to climb into the small craft, ignoring him, as part of the game they played with each other.

'I'll see you in the morning,' he said. The shuttle door closed.

The pilot started the engines. Zarifah sat by the window and looked out. Her stomach twisted in fear. She hadn't been further than the scrap heap where they scavenged, not since she was brought here. And in the fading light of the day all she could see was pile after pile of waste, metal twisted out of shape, discarded as worthless by those with new money. But it was something useable for those who were forced to live on this dying planet. Occasionally there was a small landing hut, crudely constructed from the scrap metal, indicating that there may be a House down there. Other crafts littered the sky, full of patrons coming from the bigger ships that orbited the Earth. No one landed here if they didn't have to. Yet they still came to drink and dance away their despair.

Zarifah gripped the sides of the craft as it wobbled in the air, her stomach tightened with each movement it made

'Not used to travelling,' said the old pilot, who wore the markings of the wolf, Nigil's House, on his one piece blue suit. He too had a crystal around his neck. She held her breath as he deliberately rocked the shuttle from side to side, laughing.

'Been a while.' She held her breath. She'd never been sick on the ship with her dad. But that had been many years ago. She pushed the betrayal of her father away back into the blackness of her mind.

After a twenty minute trip the engines were powered down as the pilot brought the craft to the landing platform. A distorted angel creature showed the mark of Angel House near the landing.

Sentinel Mosan struggled to unfold his legs and practically fell out of the craft into the dark corridor of Kade's House. Zarifah followed slowly. Her stomach seemed to want to go in a different direction to her body, and she was grateful that Sentinel Mosan held her arm while she got her footing and her vision stabilised and stopped swaying in sympathy with her stomach.

'Soul Dancer Zarifah, my pleasure.' A man stepped forward, holding out his hand. She took it and kissed it, keeping her eyes low, away from whom she assumed was Kade.

'This way.' Kade snapped his fingers and his own Sentinel stepped forward from the darkness and walked behind them.

Zarifah tried to take note of the corridors they walked through to get to the performance area, but the queasiness from the shuttle and her nerves, clouded her mind. *Her help me.*

Kade House was smaller than Nigil's, and a handful of dancers stood side stage, waiting to begin the harvest. Their eyes showed the hatefulness towards a Soul Dancer from another House performing on their territory. The dancers wore skimpy costumes revealing skin thick with scars. Each wore a soul crystal around their neck.

'Zarifah is our guest, you are to treat her well.' Kade had a small whip clipped to his belt. Not one of his dancers flinched. They stood emotionless. Zarifah tried to pick who was their Soul Dancer, though not all Houses had such a distinguished dancer, but she couldn't be sure.

Kade turned and clicked two empty crystals around the chain on her neck. They were a light pink and different to the crystals Nigil used. Cold, empty, and heavy. She shivered. *I will do this. I will get my ten flowers.*

'You are to harvest something worth your being here. Forget anger, fear, I want something more valuable.' The edge on his voice made her skin prickle. Sentinel Mosan kept close by, but Kade could've easily stabbed a knife into her.

'Now I'll leave you with the others, to get acquainted.'

Zarifah glanced at the other dancers. They were like a pack of wolves ready to pounce on their prey. *May Her remember the sacrifices I make.*

'Don't think we're here for you,' said one girl, dark make-up around her eyes, her costume velvet-like material covered in oddly shaped pieces of metal dangling over her brown skin.

'If you don't make the harvest tonight, it's us he'll take it out on,' said a young man and he turned so she could see the fresh red marks on his back.

'You have many patrons?' Zarifah asked coolly.

'What makes you think we'll help you,' said a blonde in a costume trimmed with red transparent material from her waist to barely cover the meeting of her thighs.

'You'll be punished if you don't,' said Zarifah. The blonde circled Zarifah as she spoke tracing her finger around her tattoo of forget-me-not flowers.

'Things aren't so posh here.' She stepped away showing her line of tattoos of thorns, oddly shaped and lines bleeding into her skin. 'But what would you do with freedom anyway? Eat the rubbish if you survive long enough on the surface to find it.' She pricked her elongated nail into Zarifah's skin causing her to gasp.

'I wonder if she could dance with broken toes,' asked

another woman approaching and stepped on Zarifah's foot. 'Like us, you wouldn't have a choice.'

'There's plenty of choice, even for us who are forced to harvest.' Zarifah tried to push the woman away.

'Whichever means less broken nails,' said the blonde. 'Levana, we could have so much fun together with this one.' The two looked similar, like twins.

'Yes, but then I don't pay like the patrons, so you'd be wasting your time,' said Zarifah wondering why Sentinel Mosan just stood there.

'Levana and Thalia, that's enough,' said a young man who had a mismatch of tattoos on his waist, making it look more like the dumping grounds outside than artwork. 'We may actually learn something from this one.'

'Nah, she's still unyielding to my touch,' said Thalia. 'And too pale, our customers are used to our darker skin.'

'Come let me have a go,' he said as he traced his finger around the nape of Zarifah's neck and her crystal.

'Really you are wasting your time.' Zarifah held her resolve. *Think of Torin. Think of what life will be like when Her walks on Earth with us again.*

'You sure are, Sanori,' said Thalia.

'Hmmm, maybe things aren't so posh after all over in your house, but you may want to brace yourself for the likes of our patrons.' He leaned over to her ear and whispered, 'Their favourite colour is red.'

'You have drummers?' asked Zarifah ignoring his words.

'No, electric music, string-like and deep,' answered the young man as he held the blonde close to him.

'And whose place am I taking tonight?'

'Mine,' he answered.

'I'm not...'

'Of course, it's the way of the future.' He pushed Levana aside. 'Without Her.'

'You still believe?' Zarifah answered, her heart now beating faster with a hope that there were other Houses that could help.

He nodded. His brown eyes engaged hers. Could he be trusted? *I could run two Houses. That would be better. More dancers would be free then.* The energy of Her in this House vibrated weaker than what she was used to. Her heart slowed, unusually so, and now she didn't know whether to even trust herself.

'Right, first dancers up,' said a male dwarf. 'Get ready.' He waddled to the front of the stage.

Sanori kept looking at Zarifah as if searching for answers that she wanted to keep to herself, to reveal when not drugged and not having to play out Nigil's games. She nodded briefly. *A risk to meet a risk.* He led her to the side of the stage.

'Always good to find out if other Houses are still worshipping Her.' His hands lingered on her shoulders. 'But even so, watching is all the help you'll get here.' He joined the dancers on the stage as the electric flute began to echo notes over the voice of the dwarf.

Their stage was slightly bigger, the patrons were just as black and dirty and while the dancers of the Angel House began to stretch their bodies to the fluid notes of the flute,

Zarifah breathed deeply trying to smell something worth hunting tonight. Anger was plenty, not much fear. She breathed again as the dancers began to work the audience to release their emotions.

And then she smelled it.

The hint of spiciness gently tickled her nose and begging her to follow. Her blood pulsed with eagerness, a longing to go out and dance now so she could taste the richness of happiness once more.

She twisted her fingers as the dancers stretched and isolated parts of their bodies to move to the notes of the flute. She should be listening to the music, trying to attune herself before going out there, to dance with unfamiliar territory.

The dance finished and fresh dancers went out on to the stage, now an electric drum and guitar-like instrument filtered out from the speakers.

'You getting a feel of this place?' asked Kade's Soul Dancer, his skin glistening a little with sweat.

Zarifah nodded and the energy of the room changed as the new dancers began to loosen up the patrons to be lost within a trance. Slowly the air became heavier with their emotions, from those who were free to express them.

Zarifah looked into the audience, trying to find the source. She'd never picked up such a faint smell so early in the night. Normally she would have to be on the stage already dancing and relying on the previous dancers to have softened the patron's awareness with the help of the House liquor. Her imprisoned soul hummed through the crystal in excitement at the prospect of what lay out there in the darkness for her to find. *Happiness*.

The dark and smoky room made it difficult for Zarifah to distinguish the patrons and it was only her nose that could detect the smell. So she waited, twisting her fingers in time with the music, watching for familiar movements of the dancers on the stage. No matter how much she tried she couldn't get her mind to work. *I want to taste happiness tonight.*

When the dwarf came back on stage it was finally her turn and with hesitant steps, she walked onto the stage behind the curtains.

Zarifah almost lost herself in the spicy smell once more. Her stomach twisted as if starved.

The dwarf had the audience pumped and they were whistling as he walked from the door and the curtain opened. The electric flute sounded individual notes as Zarifah's hips gently moved from side to side. She made the adjustment easily to the harsher sounding music. She swept her arms up, moving her fake wings and the audience slowly silenced as they became aware of the new dancer and then quickly began losing themselves in her fantasy.

For once she didn't even bother to worry if the other dancers by her side were keeping up with her rhythm but just moved with the music, trying to detect the source of the happiness in the audience. Drawn to the left, she forced herself to stay put, moving her chest in circles, teasing the patrons.

Each breath of the heavy air was so full of all sorts of emotion she thought she would choke. But when she exhaled, the air was lighter and some of the emotions were being kept inside of her. Zarifah nearly choked from the heaviness. The emotions kept within her would bind with the drug and begin to make it less potent.

In the darkest corner sat the patron who hummed with happiness. With each step closer her heart jumped a beat.

With the grace of years of experience, Zarifah moved to the patron, and smiled when she saw the female Breather once more. She focussed on tasting the happiness. Her hips made small circular movements and the eyes of the Breather followed her movements as Zarifah rippled her energy upwards from her hips, undulating her muscles and bouncing the energy between her shoulders and then back down once more.

Then the spiciness encircled Zarifah as she teased the Breather. Despite all the deep breathing she'd done, she realised how difficult this was going to be to make the extraction without wanting the energy for herself.

Coming from behind the Breather, she settled herself in front on her knees, stretching up, coaxing the happiness out. The empty crystals were just about screaming to her to be filled with this luxury. As the spicy energy filtered out of the Breather, she filled her own secret crystal first, before directing the energy to the others.

But as the Breather began to become more aware of the loss, Zarifah had misjudged this harvest. Backing off a little, she stood, slowing the energy to a standstill.

The lips of the Breather were slippery and tasteless and she pushed nearly all of herself down into the Breather in an attempt to take just a little more happiness, filling the crystals around her neck. But then as their lips began to move together, she struggled to find her way back. *I must have my payment. I need to finish my belt.*

She'd taken something the Breather was now missing and the alien latched onto her lips keeping them locked together, Zarifah unable to pull herself out and finish the harvest. She risked losing all of the happiness, for if the Breather pulled away now the spicy energy would follow and flow back.

The Breather's tongue harsh and rough as if it were grazing the insides of her mouth. And they began their own struggle as the flute music began to fade. Yet no matter how hard Zarifah tried, she couldn't pull apart from the alien, not without finishing the harvest, she would hold onto this happiness even though she wasn't going to keep it all.

Zarifah struggled to keep herself from melding with the Breather's soul. In an act of desperation she pushed some of the happiness back down into the alien, leaving the crystals around her neck only partially full of emotion. Her awareness snapped back into her body and she rushed away from the alien. Her breath came heavy. *That was close.*

13

'Risky.' Kade clipped off the crystals from her neck, smelling them himself before handing them to an Alchemist who quickly ran off to check the purity. 'Nigil said you were good, but that was dangerous, my love.' His hands ran along her bare skin from her neck to her waist.

Zarifah stood silently at the side of the stage, knowing all too well the game being played. Her energy was spent and she wanted to return back to the Wolf House and sleep, preferably in the arms of Torin.

Zarifah held her breath. Her senses were overloaded and she could smell everyone's emotion in the room, even the diluted emotions, and her mind was beginning to swell with the overload of fumes.

'Seventy per cent,' said the Alchemist.

'Disappointing.' Kade dug his fingers into her skin. 'But fortunately someone else is prepared to take a risk.'

'Flann will take you to a room. There's a client waiting for you, one who paid a lot of money, not enough to make up for an incomplete harvest, but enough that I can punish you if you're not able to pleasure her.' He pressed himself onto her body, his face meeting hers and he breathed in the lingering spicy scent. 'You will at least smell good for the patron. You disappoint this client and you'll stay forever.'

Zarifah swallowed any words of defiance. 'I'll please the client.' The ten flower payment was her motivation. She followed him past a number of doors. At the end of the corridor, Flann opened a door. He tilted his head signalling Zarifah to go in.

'Wait here, I'll be fine,' she said to Sentinel Mosan.

Zarifah stepped hesitantly to the centre of the room where the client lay in between black velvet cushions. Electric candles kept the light in the room moody and material of deep purples and blacks were hung from the ceiling. Carpet covered the floor, was soft on Zarifah's bare feet. With confidence born from experience she knelt near the person and waited to be acknowledged.

I know that scent. Zarifah shivered.

'That Breather was so happy even in a place like this. You looked so good trying to take it away from her.' Zarifah kept her head down not wanting to see Senara. 'Come here, I'm hungry and you are going to make me happy in so many ways.'

'How did you…' Zarifah moved closer to the female and looked into the familiar emotionless eyes. Zarifah was already covered in goosebumps.

'Well, let's say I'm in charge now. After meeting you, I knew what I could taste. I just had to put a few things in place, like threatening to close the Angel House, and making sure there was someone here who held an emotion worth harvesting.' Her fingers began to unlace Zarifah's belt.

'And you smell.' She inhaled deeply. 'Just like I'd wanted you to, but so much stronger.'

Zarifah surrendered what little emotions her body had to feed the client. Her mind kept turning to Torin. *Can we ever be together?* She knew the answer as emotion sucked away from her being. And it echoed painfully inside of her.

***

Senara snored gently as Zarifah lifted the woman's arm from her body. Senara stirred and opened her eyes. Zarifah stroked Senara's hair thinking what trade this woman had set up against her own kind, or maybe it was just to advance herself. *Whatever it was, it was dangerous. And I'm involved whether I like it or not.*

'Will I see you again?' asked Zarifah.

'That's for me to know.' She sat up pushing Zarifah away gently. 'Maybe I'll tire of you.'

Zarifah bowed her head. *Just pay me well for tonight.*

'You should go.' Senara waved her away.

Zarifah moved away and collected her clothes and dressed.

'We're going to be great together,' said Senara slipping on her shirt.

Zarifah looked at her, surprised. 'What do you mean?'

'A masterful plan. I'll bring you patrons worth harvesting

from, and you and I can then spend some time together. Wouldn't you want to taste more happiness?'

'Yes,' she whispered not wanting to show her need for the emotion, a need that burned in her mind harder each day she went without. Her mouth watered. To be able to taste happiness sent her mind in a spin and tangled her thoughts.

Senara brushed her fingers down Zarifah's face. 'You know if something was to happen to the current Collector, I would ensure you would take his place.'

Zarifah's widened her eyes. Her breath caught in her throat. The chance to have so much power caused a wave of dizziness to wash over her. 'Really?'

'Yes. Of course if you think to cross me I'll leave you on the surface to die.' Her fingers stopped around Zarifah's neck and she pressed dangerously hard as she kissed the Soul Dancer.

Zarifah struggled to hold onto any of her emotions as Senara sucked them from her with an unexpected force. This was what she was working towards with Her. *Can I trust her?* Senara's fingers bruised her skin releasing a wave of fear that the Regulator consumed greedily.

'Kade will be keen to know how the night went.' She released Zarifah and walked to the door. 'Let's see, shall I say you pleased me or not?' Zarifah, bowed her head. The reminder of her position stung. *Her help me.*

***

Flann escorted Zarifah from the meeting rooms in the belly of the House. Sentinel Mosan lumbered behind, not that she felt any safer with him there. The air in the corridor was stuffy but fresher than the room and her head began clearing.

'We will be seeing more of each other,' said Flann. He wore a dark blue suit and matching bow tie. His shaved head shined under the fluoro lights.

'The deal is over. I've fulfilled my duty,' said Zarifah as she tried to suppress the nauseating feeling emerging from her gut. *Nigil is a lying prick.* She glared at Flann. He laughed.

'The deal has only just begun and you have such a talent.' He ran his hands around her belt and Zarifah resisted the urge to pull away. She prayed he wouldn't feel the crystal. Now full, it hummed gently with happiness.

'I will enjoy seeing you so much more.' He went to kiss her.

'Flann!' Sanori rushed up to them. 'There's trouble down at the docks.'

'I will taste you later,' said Flann angrily as his lips brushed hers and he forced himself to pull away.

'Take our guests to The Collector, Sanori, and don't let them out of your sight. Especially her.' Flann hurried away into the shadows of the House.

'This way,' said Sanori his voice now calmer. He led them back through the upper levels.

Zarifah swayed with exhaustion herself. Sanori grabbed her around the waist and took her weight. For a short thin man he was strong and reluctantly she leant into his body and allowed herself to rest. She wanted to leave now. The idea of having to come back here, regularly, drained the last of her energy and muddled her mind.

'Aw, honey, I won't hurt you,' said Sanori quietly.

'Girlfriend's left you already Sanori, you just can't keep them long,' said a nearby dancer dressed in a skimpy black plastic material. There were smirks from the few dancers.

'Come here and say that, you weakling,' said Sanori.

'Take me to see The Collector now,' said Zarifah.

'The bitch thinks she can jump ahead,' said a male dancer.

'Nah, you have to wait like the rest of the shits in this place,' said another.

'Your girlfriend thinks she's a queen, let me teach her a lesson.' A male dancer came forth. He moved closer and swung a deliberate punch in Zarifah's face. A familiar sickening sound echoed around her as she collapsed to the ground. The Sentinel finally sprang into action.

'You're not the Soul Dancer here, you have no special treatment,' said another male dancer. 'You can wait.'

Zarifah took a deep breath. She was used to being in charge, now at this House she was at the bottom and she hated every second here. Her chest contracted and she wished to dress in a loose fitting costume. Besides, her wings had been damaged from the night and were an added weight her body refused to now carry. But she couldn't take them off without having to stand naked, not that it would really matter, she felt naked enough.

'You made a harvest tonight?' he asked. Zarifah nodded as she stepped one place forward as another entered to deliver their harvest.

'You'll need a friend here,' he said quietly as he lifted her from the ground. 'I know you'll be back. I don't want you here, but things will go so much more smoothly if we work together.'

'I work alone. I am the Soul Dancer…'

'Not here. Life is hell here more so than what you are used to. The scars still healing on your back are nothing to the scars the dancers of this House bear in their minds. No one has ever danced here and left.'

'You don't want to be here,' said Zarifah as she tried to keep her mind away from the stars and the blackness that was demanding to overtake her. 'I can't trust you.'

'I don't want you here either. Look at the trouble you have caused outside just by your presence.' A gun blast sounded above the yelling and punching. No one screamed at the metallic sound. But now there were different sounds that Zarifah tried to block out. The blasts came closer. Sentinel Mosan pushed Zarifah aside. It happened quickly. A sharp pain exploded in Zarifah's face and she stumbled back with a scream. Sentinel Mosan stood in front of her, but then suddenly fell, blood pooling on the floor from a chest wound. Sanori grabbed Zarifah and pulled her through a door.

'Are you okay?' Guns fired outside.

Zarifah nodded. 'What's going on?'

'Trouble with a patron.'

It suddenly went quiet outside. Kade walked in. 'You should've stopped them.' He slammed the door. He paused looking at Zarifah and Sanori, the veins on his neck stood out.

'At least your patron was happy with you.' He glared at

Sanori. 'You had better have a word with Thalia.' Kade stepped further into the room. 'Now.'

Sanori scrambled to leave before being told again.

'You're now free to go,' Kade said. 'I will arrange with Nigil for you to return next month.'

'Like that will happen when he sees my face.' Zarifah pushed herself to a sitting position. The room spun suddenly one way and then the other and she held her breath against the rising bile in her throat.

'We'll see.' He pulled her up from the ground. 'Now there's a small problem about your Sentinel so you are going to have to walk by yourself.'

'Nigil won't be happy,' said Zarifah, staggering out of the room after him.

'He is only a Sentinel. Part of our business down here, isn't it?' He kept moving quickly and Zarifah struggled to keep pace. Her head throbbed.

'Always messy down here.' Kade kept moving confidently down the maze of corridors to the docking area. 'That Regulator was rather helpful. Especially when I told her that she could see you again.' He turned to watch her expression.

'You had no right to promise me to anyone.' Zarifah's words short as she struggled for breath.

'Always defiant. You waste so much energy when you are like that.' He stopped at the loading bay. Zarifah climbed into her ship, stars at the edge of her vision.

'I'll be seeing you soon.'

14

Nigil stormed back and forth behind his desk. He went to punch his desk but managed to stop himself.

'The rotten lying son of...' Nigil growled out his anger once more. Zarifah, tired and barely managing to keep awake, sat in front of his desk. Her head thumped continuously. Zarifah tried not to look at the door to the Alchemists. The full crystal pulsed gently, like ripples of tickles under her belt, and she itched to go and extract her personal harvest.

Nigil's face turned red. Sweat dribbled down his forehead. 'Kade isn't going to get away with this!' This time he did lose control and slammed his fist on the metal table, just missing the console. He yelled in pain. A Sentinel quickly came into the room and went to constrain Zarifah.

'Can I go?' Zarifah shrugged off the Sentinel. 'I am sure that you can conjure a plan without my help.'

'If I find that you have conspired with Kade, I will not

hesitate to take the whip to you again.' Nigil gave her a thunderous stare.

'Would you like me to send for a Medic?' she asked coolly.

'No. Take her away, and bring me the guy downstairs in the isolation room, he can deal with my hand. Go and make sure you put some cream on your face. I want you dancing tonight.'

The Sentinel dragged her out and pushed her on her way.

Her room was as she had left it, and gratefully she lay on her bed and was about to fall asleep when someone knocked.

'Enter.' Zarifah's voice thick with sleep. She settled herself into a semi-sitting position.

'Are you all right, Zarifah?' Hayal rushed to Zarifah's side. Etana stood at the doorway staring.

'Who the hell did this to you?' demanded Torin. He pushed Hayal aside to have a closer look. Zarifah stifled a gasp as he put his finger under her chin and tilted her head to the side. His touch sparked her desires. *No one else can do something like that to me.* Her heart quickened and her muscles between her thighs convulsed with yearning for him.

'I am going to say something to Nigil,' said Torin. 'He should never have permitted you go to another House, because this is what happens at best, at worst you'd be zipped up in plastic.'

Zarifah didn't mention how close that came. *This is another reason why we can't be together. He will worry about me too much.*

'No don't say anything. It could be advantageous for our plan,' said Zarifah. 'Besides he's so angry at the moment he is likely to kill you. Truly I have never seen him lose his cool like this. I don't think he's going to be able to say no to Kade.'

'What do you mean? Kade wants you back and Nigil is going to say yes?' Torin frowned. Dark circles under his eyes told Zarifah how much he had been concerned for her while she was away. *This won't do.* But then she caught a hint of spiciness. Happiness. A different yearning opened up inside of her.

'Keep quiet, Zarifah,' said Hayal as she began lathering the cold cream on Zarifah's face. The scent of eucalyptus overpowered the spice of happiness.

'It hurts,' complained Zarifah. 'Torin, do you have something for the pain.'

'No. I think you turn to the pills too much. Besides I am finding trade difficult since the Regulators have been here. I do however have some nutrient pills for you.' Zarifah reluctantly swallowed these pills and rested back her head on the pillow.

'Have you contacted Her?' Zarifah asked as Hayal applied the last of the cream.

'Zarifah you can't talk like this in front of Etana,' said Hayal. 'Not yet, not until she has been initiated.'

'But she understands Hayal, more than anyone else her age.'

'There is plenty of time.'

'No there's not.' The increase in volume in Zarifah's voice made everyone in the room jump.

'Calm down, Zarifah,' said Hayal.

Torin handed her an orange pill, perfectly round with a

flower stamped on the centre. 'This is my last.' He kissed her forehead. 'Rest.' His voice soothed her.

She swallowed the pill. 'Thank you.'

'Her will understand,' said Torin.

Zarifah wasn't so sure. Time was running out for Her in the Astral plane. She needed to get control of the House soon before Her faded into nothing.

Torin stood and guided the others towards the door. 'Sleep well Soul Dancer,' he said before they left.

The door clicked shut and Zarifah spiralled into a disturbed sleep.

The energy from the Astral plane pulled Zarifah away from her nightmares, her exhausted state making it easy for her to travel in this disembodied form.

The mountain was bare and she stood in the wind, waiting and confused. She wanted to meet Her.

Zarifah wrapped her arms around her body, providing herself with little comfort against the cold wind and the moody sky. It always surprised her how much she could still feel in the etheric form, or maybe her mind was tricking her.

Her walked up to Zarifah, wings extended out; her etheric form glowed a deep red. Zarifah could see through Her's form more than usual.

'Mother.' Zarifah knelt respectfully.

'Why have you come?'

The question scattered Zarifah's thoughts. *I hadn't planned to.* Muddled, she kept her eyes downcast.

'You should been focusing on the completion of your belt, so then you'll have more freedom, which will lead to you becoming the new Collector. Nigil must die, and soon. I'm fading here. The void is tugging at my essence, causing me to unravel. If you waste any more time, I won't be able to reincarnate. I expected more from you. You had such raw talent, the strongest that we had seen for such a long time. But this *happiness* weakens you. I hope we aren't too late.'

Tears welled in Zarifah's eyes. She fought back the tears. Her's words stung. 'I'm trying. I've got an Alchemist working on reversing the soul-splitting process.'

Her didn't look impressed. 'I don't want to know about anything unless Nigil is dead and you have control of the House. I don't even want to know if you get all your tattoos because you should've finished that task already.' Her pulled herself to full height, towering over Zarifah. 'Get back down there and do what you were born to do. If I need to summon you again, I will drag your form up here.'

Zarifah found herself back in her body. It felt like she really had been prodded with pokers and she determined to make amends in case she failed. She hauled herself away from the comfort of her bed and washed, removing the last hints of spiciness. She selected black transparent harem pants with a tight black top to wear and gave her air machine a bang. As she walked from her room she tried to shake the doubt that still clouded her mind. She wanted payment on her skin straight away.

'I have more flowers to be added,' she told the Ink Master when she finally found him. Late afternoon meant that the tattooist was not in his room but elsewhere in the House doing whatever needed to be done in the old rooms. Today he was helping to fix the ropes; they had somehow been tangled and looked like a mess of knotted brown snakes.

'What the hell happened to you,' said Ink Master.

'Long night at Kade's House, some things didn't go to plan.'

'Yeah, there's been lots of whispering today. Poor Sentinel Mosan, I didn't mind him. And The Collector, well he has been in such a foul mood, he had hit at least two people and probably broken his hand.'

'Blue forget-me-nots, right? Let's get them done so you can dance with pride in your own House tonight. Thank Her that you didn't get inked at Kade's.' He left the ropes.

'Yeah, you should've seen the shoddy work there, ink blobs which were near uncountable,' said Zarifah. They walked to the tattoo room and with well-practised hands, Ink Master began to set up the machine.

'How many?' he asked.

'Ten.' The Ink Master whistled as Zarifah handed over her chip and lay on the bench.

'How many left?'

'Hmm, 14.' *So close.* For the first time her freedom was becoming a reality and the plan with her would soon start.

They heard Nigil yelling at one of the Sentinels further down the corridor and Zarifah prayed to Her that he wouldn't come in.

'Let's see your face?' Nigil strode into the room. 'Wear a mask. And you really could've had the tattoos done later, or are you planning on not harvesting tonight?'

Zarifah just stared at him not wanting to provoke him and

cause her already swollen face to be hit again, something he was more than capable of doing at the moment. His hand was heavily bandaged and it was easy to tell he had doped himself up on painkillers.

'I am also looking forward to seeing the new dancer perform tonight. I have sent out the message and there should be a big crowd tonight. So you had better be ready.' He glanced angrily at Ink Master who had continued to work.

'You make sure you help the maintenance guys during the dances, I am starting to think that you are getting an easy ride here Ink Master. Might even have to promote you to Sentinel status, if I don't find a replacement, though your muscles are most definitely not your assets.'

'Collector, the new Sentinel is here,' said a man from the door.

'Right, let's see what dirt bags have a need to bargain. I do hate it when I have to trade money for Sentinels, such a waste.' Nigil walked out of the room.

'He wouldn't really make you a Sentinel,' said Zarifah.

'No, fortunately Her made me thin like a boy and no matter what I take there is no bulking up this body.' Ink Master laughed to himself. 'Even if The Collector got desperate, the bad guys would take one look at me and take me on knowing they would win.'

'Maybe you would have more muscles if you were dancing again,' said Zarifah.

'Not that line again, Zarifah.' He made some final brushes with the electric needles. 'There done.'

Zarifah sat up and slipped off the table.

'Don't get into any mischief tonight, Zarifah,' he said.

'No of course not,' said Zarifah and with a wink, left the man to clean up the needles ready for the onslaught after the packed house Nigil had organised for tonight.

With a throbbing face, she walked into the practice room. It was nearly time for the dancers to start preparing for the nightly performance.

'Don't even bother telling me that I look like shit,' said Zarifah when Torin approached her.

'Nigil wants a new dancer to start tonight,' said Torin. Black lines made his eyes appear more sunken. 'Malkia is ready.'

'You don't look so good yourself.'

'Yeah, well don't worry your pretty head about me.' But Zarifah was curious about what he was up to.

'Let me see her dance.' She bit her tongue to stop herself from asking him for more pills. He had given her the last the night before. Maybe she needed to try and do some trading of her own down here. Shuttles came and went often enough and if you wanted, things could be smuggled in and out. Though as Soul Dancer she always thought that her presence at or near the docking area would draw too much attention. It would never work. Besides she now had access, basically free range of the Alchemist rooms. *I should go there soon.*

Malkia's thin young body moved with the music and she gave an almost perfect technical performance. But she was lacking some deeper feeling in her movements, an energy connection to herself which was needed for the harvesting. Perhaps Malkia would improve this connection with experience. *Or maybe she just isn't ever going to manage to complete a harvest.* And Nigil wouldn't be happy to hear that.

'Malkia darling, go and get ready for tonight. The patrons will just love you,' said Zarifah. *Well there were always the other options for this girl.* 'Hayal, can you help her get ready?' Hayal nodded and took the girl away.

'And there, just like that, we send another to the belly of the devil and not to the gracious arms of Her,' said Torin.

'Have you visited Her lately? Her arms are hardly gracious,' said Zarifah. 'Do you think she is lacking ability because we have been disconnected to Her, to the Earth for these many years?' asked Zarifah to Torin.

He slipped his hand around her waist and drew her in close. 'Or maybe the skills of the younglings are weakening because they don't have the connection with Her.'

'We are running out of time.'

'Yes, but don't you have a plan? One which you really should trust me with.' His muscles contracted around her in an embrace. The desire to lose herself in his arms, in his strength and forget about everything in this hell hole, even the hope of making a difference. And then as she inhaled to speak, she noticed the tainted smell. She inhaled again as Torin squeezed her. Ever so weak, ever so desirable, the smell cinnamon. The empty crystals around her neck cried at the inability to harvest such happiness. Zarifah resisted the urge to kiss him, but not the usual empty kisses she gave, one that was more passionate, more real. Her lips tingled, wanted to touch his but she held back.

'I think that you harvested some extra things when you

were away,' said Torin quietly. 'So are you going to share with me?' His breath was hot on her ears and the spicy smell intensified.

'If I can transfer it to a form that is able to be used.'

'Then I will visit you tonight. After all, I don't have any more pills and the only shuttles coming here today are not the usual trade, I haven't been able to replenish my stock.'

The spicy smell of happiness fogged the edges of her mind and she struggled to keep control. 'Good.'

He brushed his lips over her cheek in a series of butterfly kisses, moving down her neck. Her body shivered in pleasure and the spicy scent filled the air between them.

I've got to get out of here. Zarifah pushed him away. Her legs were weak and barely obeyed the commands of her mind as she walked away from the scent. *Can I trust him? Her guide me.* The scent called her back. And it took all her strength to keep walking away.

15

Zarifah threw the mask on the ground and then kicked it across her room. She couldn't manage to change it how she would like to, so that it would cover all her bruises and still look appealing. It was a white mask, lined with gold.

Finally she pulled some red feathers off an old costume and attached them with synthetic clear thread onto the sides of the mask. Both her eyes and her cheeks would be covered with the feathers. Zarifah didn't think that it looked appealing, but time was running out and there was nothing else that she could do. Her fingers worked rapidly from years of experience.

Standing in front of the full length mirror, one that extended out from a tiny gap between storage compartments, she reviewed her costume with a critical eye. Black marks on the mirror made it difficult to see properly, but at least she had a mirror. Once again she ran her fingers over her belt. The crystal, full of happiness, pulsed waiting to be emptied. She had secured it between the layers of material and planned to visit Oren tonight.

Zarifah's plaited hair hung down her back. A simple white slinky bodice, lined with delicate gold-looking interlocking loops created a false armour around her chest. She placed some metal bands around her biceps. She took care with her appearance, applying kohl to her eyes with a steady hand, and double checking her reflection in the mirror to make sure her hair was in place as well as her costume.

The electric bell buzzed, signalling for the dancers to move to the stage area for the night's performance. Sliding the mirror away, Zarifah prayed to Her before joining the other dancers. The corridors looked darker than usual and the concrete floor warm underfoot; the air coolers struggled to remove the heat in the warren.

Malkia stood next to two other younger dancers, her teenage body trembling sporadically.

'Malkia darling, you will do Her proud,' Zarifah whispered in the girl's ear as she gave her a cold hug.

The Presenter was on the stage preparing the crowd. Through the peepholes in the metal boards, Zarifah saw that the patrons were again low in numbers tonight. Nigil wandered between the members like a caged lion, offering free alcohol to loosen their emotions. *He must be hurting to do that.* Her blood ran a little cooler when she saw Kade. He was the last person she'd expect to see tonight.

Zarifah fidgeted side stage as Malkia began her first harvest. Instead she mentally calculated how much time she had until her dance and, looking into the audience, she found Nigil. *Good, he's busy.*

'You leaving?' said Torin as he grabbed her arm tightly.

'Yes, and you promised that you'll not interfere, and cover my absence,' said Zarifah.

'Don't get yourself killed,' said Torin and he unexpectedly kissed her. Zarifah's body weakened and the scent of cinnamon from his breath flowed to hers. 'So go,' he said when he finally released her. Zarifah hurried away before changing her mind. The smell of happiness chased her. Zarifah slipped into Nigil's office.

Zarifah held her breath again as she swiped the chip for entrance to the Alchemist's room. Walking in with a little less confidence, she scanned the room. Empty. She took out the crystal and placed it in the box like Oren had shown her.

She wasn't sure if she had set up the machine correctly, but she pushed the button anyway and waited and prayed to Her. Just as she was putting the empty crystal back into her belt with the phial of happiness, a movement to her left caught her attention.

'I was wondering when you would be back. I've missed you,' said Oren. Dark shadows ringed under his eyes from long working hours.

'Honey, I am sure that you did,' said Zarifah as she slipped her hands around his neck. 'But you know how dangerous it is for me to be here, and that if I stay with you someone will come looking for me.' She stroked his thinning blond hair. 'And you know how angry The Collector has been.'

'Yes, well, I won't take long.' He tried to kiss her.

'Business first,' said Zarifah as she pulled away. 'Can you show me how to re-join the souls?'

'Well…' He looked hungrily at Zarifah.

'Honey, this is a silent war, you have to stay focussed.' He was wasting her time and she had to get back to the stage soon.

'Nearly, at the moment there is some fragmenting when the soul is reunited. But with some fine tuning of the energy with electrics and magnetic fields this should be overcome.'

'There is a but?' She crossed her arms.

'There will be no guarantee. Some souls will reunite and others will fragment. There is no way of knowing what will happen.'

'What have you been practising on?'

'Katners.'

Zarifah wrinkled her face in disgust. 'I didn't think that they had souls?'

'Well I guess they do, or maybe that's some of the problem.'

'So the next step?' Her patience thinned.

'I can fine tune a little more…'

'How long will that take?' Zarifah frowned at him. The pressure from the goddess telling her to hurry up weighed on her shoulders.

'A month or so.'

'Then?'

'We can start testing on humans.'

'Right then, you have a week.' Who should she test this out

on first. *Nigil.* But that would be a waste because Her didn't want him to live.

'But what if I'm not ready?' His hands fidgeted with his soul crystal around his neck.

'Well then that person may die. Would you feel responsible?'

'Yes.'

'Work hard then.' The anger in her voice caused him to flinch.

'I expect to see progress next time I visit, I would like a demonstration on one of those rats.'

'Okay, but what about me.' The hunger in his eyes returned. Zarifah was about to rush out the door when she remembered that she had all but used Torin's stock.

'You have any red pills, or orange pills?' asked Zarifah. Oren nodded. 'Get me some.'

Oren disappeared through a glass door for a while and came back with a small box, he opened it to show that it was full of the pills she asked for.

'Now for my pleasure,' he said.

Zarifah held up her hand and stopped him. 'If I'm not back at the stage now, who do you think will be punished?'

He swallowed hard. 'Later then.'

Zarifah left him with no intention of giving him anything. She hurried to the stage.

'Soul Dancer!' yelled a Sentinel. 'You are meant to be dancing.'

'As you can see I am on my way.' Zarifah adjusted her costume to ensure the empty crystal in her belt was secure, along with the small box now hidden in the folds of material wrapped around her chest.

'Hayal and Torin are just beginning, go out now.'

Without any thought, Zarifah danced onto the stage between Hayal and Torin in a dramatic entrance. Her costume glowed white, absorbing the little light on the stage making her look larger. The eyes of the patrons turned to her, their hunger like invisible biting insects. Zarifah breathed deeply, automatically hunting for something worth harvesting. But for now there was only the usual stench in the room.

Fortunately the harvest dance hadn't started. Torin looked relieved to see her.

'Ready?' Zarifah asked. She already found it difficult to concentrate with Torin walking onto the stage with her. All through the dance she struggled to keep her focus, her mind wandering to Torin, her lips tingled with the memory of the kiss, and her body ached with the desire for more.

Breathing deeply, she smelt the spiciness and her knees went weak and she struggled to stand and complete the harvest. Looking around, she saw the source. Her eyes rested on Torin. Using all her strength, she danced further away, but it was like her whole body was in tune with this spicy smell. It was like she had to have that emotion pulsing through her veins, all the time.

Zarifah struggled to finish the dance as soon as Torin came closer, but the scent didn't become strong, it was only teasing her. She had to have more. But she held her resolve.

Frustration burned inside of her and shortened her patience. Zarifah stepped off the stage and tried to catch her breath.

'Soul Dancer, it's Malkia, the new one who performed tonight.' The Sentinel looked pale and stressed.

'Fuck. Where is she?' said Zarifah.

'In the dorms, two of the men are holding her down,' said the Sentinel.

Zarifah forgot about the argument and ran to the dormitories. Hayal and Torin followed. This sometimes happened. Their first dance somehow cemented the split between the souls and if they remembered Her they were also reminded they were no longer connected to the source.

The howling from the girl could be heard in the corridors like a haunting echo. Each scream bounced off the metal walls and intensified. Some of the other dancers stood outside, fingers in their ears, trying not to remember what they themselves went through.

Malkia thrashed her arms and legs as if they were weapons and the thin dancer somehow gained strength and the men struggled to hold her. Blood dribbled down their faces and arms, signs of her success.

'She's reacting to the harvest.' Zarifah tried slapping the girl, trying to shock her out of the outburst but she continued howling and thrashing, her words incomprehensible but loud and haunting to those who heard. *Her help us.*

'Hayal, fill a bath with cold water,' said Zarifah.

'Do you want some drugs?' asked Torin.

'Not yet, it will be better if she doesn't have the drugs. Let's drag her down to the showering area and put her in the cold bath.' The men struggled to carry the young girl as she thrashed.

'Go and rest,' yelled Zarifah to some of the dancers who were standing around watching as they entered the washrooms. A tub was being filled with water.

'They just wanted to help,' said Torin.

'Watching isn't helping.' Zarifah was finding it difficult to hear over the continuous screaming of the girl.

The men lowered Malkia in and held her down. The shock of suddenly being cold stopped the screaming and thrashing. Everyone in the room let out a sigh of relief. But then the screaming started again.

'Hold her, don't let her harm herself,' said Zarifah. The girl had scratched her face and arms, but someone must have recognised what was going on and stopped her before she could do permanent damage to herself.

The tension rose in the room once more with the continual howling. The words were less audible now, and the girl's voice was slowly becoming weaker, but still she wouldn't let up.

'It's not working, Zarifah,' said Hayal sobbing.

'Drugs are the only option,' said Torin. 'Zarifah, we've given her a chance, we have to look after ourselves.'

'Get The Collector,' said Zarifah to Hayal. Her chances of recovering were now low. *Very low.* Zarifah clenched her jaw tight. *Hurry up please.* Each screech from Malkia tore at her own soul.

'Fuck.' Nigil moved by the side of the tub. 'Hold her.' He

had the syringe ready, full of yellow liquid, which he pumped straight into her arm muscle.

'Keep an eye on her and if she needs more, send for me. I will not have her screams disturbing the others,' grumbled Nigil. He looked coolly at Zarifah. 'If she doesn't recover, I'll have her sold.'

Zarifah struggled to keep his stare. One that made her blame herself for what was happening. *I should've followed Her's instructions faster. If I were in charge, Malkia wouldn't have danced tonight.* She took a deep breath. *This is my fault.*

16

Zarifah removed her costume and dressed in loose pants and a tight thin strapped blue top. She concealed the crystal in the blue material around her torso. Zarifah wanted to collect the crystal now, but she didn't relish the idea of seeing Oren again. *Her keep Malkia safe.* The guilt stabbed at her belly, the emotion swirled around her clouding her judgement. Wincing, Zarifah wiped more cream over her face. *Will Torin come?* After what had happened with Malkia she supposed it would be too much to ask. Most dancers would be hiding in their rooms tonight trying to forget about the screams and the reminder of when their own souls were split. She had her way of dealing with this. A phial of happiness under her pillow ready to drink. *It will keep the nightmares away.*

Zarifah nearly missed the quiet knock on the door. She smiled as Torin entered.

'Well you were helpful tonight,' said Zarifah.

'You nearly missed the harvest. What the hell are you

playing at.' He pinched her arm causing her to grimace. 'Tell me now.'

Zarifah told him what happened at the Angel's House. About the Breather and Senara and the proposition that was made to her.

'So I guess you are going to somehow use Senara in your plan,' said Torin his forehead wrinkled in thought.

'Yeah, but I'm not sure how yet, though I am sure she'll be useful.'

'Not as useful as you to her. She sucked you dry of any sort of emotions each time you saw her. Look at you now, you're exhausted and not eating.'

The spicy scent thickened between them.

'Do you smell that?' asked Zarifah. Torin nodded, leaned over and kissed her.

'Wait, there's something I want to try.' Zarifah took out the phial of happiness from under her pillow.

'Zarifah, I don't know about this,' said Torin as he tenderly caressed her belly.

'I want to know what will happen if I drink this. It's food to the Emotionless, not us?'

She unstoppered the phial, the clear liquid, now mature, was odourless and tasteless. 'Do you want half?'

'Fuck. This is dangerous.' He pursed his lips together. 'Of course, give me half.' Torin winked.

Zarifah knew he wouldn't be able to resist and smiled. She drank the colourless liquid and handed the phial to him. He drank the remaining liquid as if it was a shot of Spirit.

'Now, we were doing some rather delicate exploring,' said

Torin and he went back to kissing her neck and moving along her body. With each kiss the smell of happiness intensified and her soul vibrated with the emotion she'd drunk. The scent of cinnamon flowed between them. Soon she was moaning with pleasure from the kisses as if each were a flower that had been tickled to her skin leaving pollen cascading down like rain. Her body was soon trembling with pleasure, the happiness somehow heightened the experience. Everything that Torin did to her was more intense, and she found herself lost somewhere in the bliss while their bodies pumped to a new pulse. Together they moved and breathed and the flow went equally between them as they joined more than just their bodies and the scent wrapped around them like invisible tendrils lifting them higher and higher. Gasping together, sucking in the spiciness around them, they reached new heights of awareness. Screams of pleasure signalled their peak in unison. Spent, they spiralled back to Earth, like falling feathers as their heartbeats slowed and the smell faded. Tight in each other's embrace, they lay together out of breath. The downward spiral sent them both into a deep sleep.

Zarifah woke feeling Torin's muscular body resting on hers. Her soul wanted the night to be repeated, and called for another phial of happiness to be drunk. There was a black loss within her now. The longing caused her head to throb and her stomach to cramp. She hoped that she would be returning to Kade's house soon if that meant she could harvest happiness.

Torin stirred and gently kissed her. Zarifah's body eased

into his, savouring his touch. Lingering cinnamon floated on the air and she breathed in deeply.

The alarm sounded, causing them both to jump and pull apart. Adrenalin pulsed through Zarifah as she grabbed for something to wear. Then she laughed. 'It's a scavenging day.'

'I was somewhere about here before the interruption.' He eased his body on the bed next to hers and nibbled at the base of her neck. Zarifah make soft sounds of pleasure, her mind clouded, but then she managed to find her resolve.

She pushed him back. 'You had better go.'

Torin resisted. 'I'm not going anywhere until I've finished what I started.'

'I don't want Nigil to see us arriving together.'

Torin grumbled as he dressed. He pulled her in his arms and brushed his lips over hers. Her knees weakened and her mind clouded pleasantly.

'Make sure you are at the gates, Zarifah.' He let her go and left. She chewed her bottom lip to stop herself from calling him back to stay. Part of her didn't care if she went scavenging or not, but then if she wanted to have Torin close, she had to.

Zarifah quickly tidied the room and placed the empty phial back in the material tied around her chest. Dressing in warm clothes, she made herself ready to go outside. She placed the box of pills Oren gave her in the pocket of her jacket, planning to give a few to Torin since he'd been so generous with his supply recently. Her face looked better, still black and blue with some dashes of yellow. She smeared on more cream and then covered her face with a scarf.

She hurried, looking forward to seeing Torin again. But she was late. The gate was already open. There was some moisture in the air, the pollution hung low below a few angry clouds smeared in the sky. There appeared to be new piles of rubbish to scavenge through and the dancers of the House hurried to those areas. The dancers from the Angel House were nearby, scavenging through the rubbish. A few yells and punches sent them back away from the spoils.

She found Torin banging on an old shuttle to scare away any katners that may have decided to use the place for a nest. A bundle of stinking black fur scampered out, hissing at Torin's legs as he danced out of its way.

'That was close,' said Zarifah. She picked through a pile of wires, chains and scrap metal.

'Come on inside,' said Torin as he fiddled with the electronics and opened the door.

'I'll let you scout inside first, there might be katners.'

Torin banged around inside the metal pod for a few seconds before announcing the all clear.

'You looking for something in particular today?' asked Torin.

'Yeah.' She went straight to the engine compartment and started pulling off the protective metal.

'Well since when do we have secrets from each other,' said Torin.

'Crystals,' she answered as she crawled part way in and started looking.

'Yeah well, you'll need to do more than pray to Her to get that.' Torin picked up the metal sheets that had been pulled off from under the navigation console. 'You know they strip the shuttles of the crystals before they are dumped.'

'Yeah, but I am praying to Her that someone got lazy, or that they had to dump in a hurry.'

'There's good bit of metal there,' said a male voice at the open hatch of the shuttle.

'Get lost, we were here first,' said Torin not even looking up from the wires he was untangling.

'This would do nicely.' The man mumbled to himself and began pulling off a sheet of metal.

'Since when did scum from the likes of your House bother talking to us,' said Torin. 'And I did tell you politely to leave, now I am going to have to get nasty. But I hear that's the way you guys like it over there.'

'Really, fighting's not going to help is it, Zarifah,' said the man.

Zarifah bumped her head at the sound of her name. She looked over her shoulder. 'Sanori. What are you doing so far away from your House?' She rubbed her head.

'We're in need of more material. Boss has given a few of us a ride in a shuttle to more suitable grounds.' He held up a handful of electrical wires.

'Yeah right,' said Torin sarcastically. He folded his arms across his chest. 'Like that's the real reason.'

Sanori shrugged and looked at Zarifah. 'Ouch, your face did get messed up.'

'What do you want? Both of us will get a whipping from our owners if we are seen talking here.'

'I'm open to a bit of trade.' Sanori looked at Torin.

'I don't have anything to trade with.' Torin's face remained stone cold. He may have the body that was toned and strong, but he was no fighter. But then neither was Sanori.

'Now come on, that's no way to treat a friend.'

'You've got no friends here.' Torin put his hands on Sanori's and the men faced off.

'Well it is appearing that way. But as Zarifah knows I believe in Her, and well if she's going to keep coming over to my end of the street then she's going to need a friend.'

'Boys, that's enough.' Zarifah moved between them.

'What have you got to trade with?' asked Zarifah.

'You first.'

'You came here, so you either show us what've you got or you leave, our time is running out and if we are all seen leaving the shuttle together we will soon be wishing we are dead.' Zarifah looked icily at Sanori.

Sanori pulled out a dirty cloth, unwrapping it with some dramatic air revealing a small collecting crystal. 'Thought that might take your fancy.'

'How did you…' Zarifah's mind began thinking as she tried not to panic at the thought he may know she harvested a little extra the other night.

'*How* is not important to you. The question is *what* do you have for me?'

'Nothing, we don't want your help,' said Torin.

Sanori raised his eyebrow.

'You should leave now,' continued Torin, but Sanori didn't move.

Zarifah pulled out the small box of pills. She was reluctant to have to trade with these but it would be easier for her to get more pills than to find more crystals.

Sanori he let out a whistle.

'Let me see the crystal.' The crystal felt dead in her hand, not heavy, just dead. This could mean that it was clean or hadn't been used much or it could mean that it was of a low quality and didn't hold the emotions within its walls. No one wanted a leaky crystal. She held it up to try and catch some light through its walls, but there wasn't much light in the shuttle and she didn't dare take the crystal outside.

'It's a dud,' said Zarifah. In truth she wasn't sure.

'Your words cut me deep.'

'Dud.' And Zarifah handed back the crystal.

'All right, I'll show you. But this will be the only time I'll be generous with you.'

'Get a move on, we don't have much time,' said Torin.

Sanori took out a small flask. It held a colourless liquid which he poured over the crystal as he hummed the beat of the harvest, coaxing the emotion held in the liquid to answer the call of the crystals. The liquid flowed into the crystal. The smell of citrus wafted around them.

'Yours, for the box of pills. You have a full crystal and will have to work out how to get the emotion out.' He held up the crystal, it pulsed a soft orange.

'Well that could be rather difficult,' said Zarifah trying to play down the exchange. *Looks like I'll have to see Oren soon.*

'Something tells me you like a challenge.' He winked as he took the pills and hid them within the layers of his clothes.

'When you're at my House don't trade. It's too risky.' And with a wink he left the shuttle.

'Charming,' said Torin. Zarifah slipped the crystal in the folds of her top. It pulsed warm against her skin.

'Zarifah help me with this bit of metal,' said Torin.

They put their body weight behind the metal to try and bend it backwards. With a groan they pulled together.

'Fuck,' yelled Torin as a black mass hurtled at his shoulder. 'Get it off.' He tried to pull the katner from his body, but it had anchored itself in his flesh with its teeth. Torin groaned in pain as Zarifah tried to hit it with a bit of sharp metal.

'Keep still or I'll cut you,' said Zarifah. The katner kept its grip and hissed. Finally the metal hit in the small body and with a scream the animal let go and Torin flung it across the pod. When the katner didn't move, Zarifah grabbed another piece of metal and speared the animal.

Torin clutched his shoulder, breathing heavily. 'Some of those pills would be bloody helpful right now.'

'Glad your twisted sense of humour is still working,' said Zarifah as she began pulling off his jacket.

'Always knew you couldn't resist me.' His voice rose as she accidently touched his wound.

'Shut up.' Zarifah pulled off her scarf and wrapped it as tightly as she could around the wound to stop the bleeding, the teeth hadn't gone in too deep, the layers of clothing had offered some weak protection. She tried to convince herself that it could've been worse, but the dirty teeth of the katner had bacteria and that could be a problem.

Encouraging Torin to lean on her, they left the pod and

began walking back to the House. Torin leant on her heavily as she tried to hold his weight while they stumbled over mounds of rubbish, back towards the House. *Her keep him safe.*

'Help us,' screamed Zarifah to the Sentinels at the gate when they were in sight. She waved frantically. 'Bloody thick skulls,' said Zarifah when no one came over. She continued yelling at them until finally one of them ran over and took the weight of Torin.

'What happened?' asked the Sentinel.

'Katner,' said Zarifah struggling to breath. 'Quickly he must be scanned and treated.'

Zarifah held her breath when the red light lit up on the scanner. The katner had left something in the wound and now he'd have to have another scan. The screen flashed the species of which bacteria had been detected—the usual. Antibodies were needed for *E.coli*, *staph*, and *pseudomonas* and the suited up Tech went into the scanning room and injected around the wound. Torin would still have to be in isolation to make sure the infection was contained. An open wound outside was likely to have picked up some parasite floating in the polluted air. Zarifah prayed to Her that the Tech would give him an injection just to make sure. They carried Torin away. She blinked back tears. It was going to be tough without him around.

'Enter.'

Zarifah walked into the room. The floor was wet from being sterilised, and she waited to be scanned. She sighed when the green light flashed on the screen, but because she had blood on her hands and clothes, she had to go to the isolation area to clean up.

Wearing nothing but a white medical gown, she quickly walked back to her room. She had concealed the crystal and phial because her clothes were going to be burnt and she was annoyed at having to begin again and scavenge for more warm clothes; that could take months.

'Trouble seems to follow you these days,' said Nigil as he met her in the corridor near her room. 'I wonder if you are really worth keeping.

'But I guess you are going to make me lots of money from going to Kade's House. I look forward to being a rich man.' He traced his finger along the gap in the back of her gown, undoing the ties at the back as he kissed her neck.

'So you have agreed?' Her body went rigid.

'Don't make me out to be the bad guy here. I do try to look after you. It's not like you make it easy for me,' he said between kisses as he began to move across her skin to her shoulder, slipping the gown down to expose her naked body.

Zarifah held her hands behind her back as he pressed his body close to hers. *Don't.* It would be another whipping if he found the crystal. Her heart thudded to an erratic beat. His aniseed breath turned her stomach.

Screams from the dormitory filtered through the corridors and sent shivers of fear along the backs of anyone who heard.

'Fuck.' Nigil hesitated, thinking about continuing to play. Zarifah knew his soul ached with the knowledge of the separation and with each echo, his own soul screamed silently. 'Maybe I will see you later,' said Nigil as he released her.

Zarifah walked back to the room, her knees weak at how close she'd been to getting caught.

17

The main harvest went well enough. Zarifah walked from the stage with the crystals full of the putrid smell of guilt pulsing around her neck. She longed for happiness.

She went straight to Nigil's office to deliver the harvest. Nigil's hand was heavily bandaged and the glazed look in his eyes suggested he had been overusing the drugs to forget the pain. He gave her one flower and Zarifah held her tongue against the low number, and about once again being given a poor deal. *Twelve and a half flowers to go.* Finishing her belt was still taking longer than she would have liked. But more importantly she still hadn't figured a way to take control of the House from Nigil. She turned to leave his office.

'You'll go back to Kade's House for another harvest at the end of the week,' said Nigil.

'It's too dangerous, look what happened last time.' The bruises on her face were fading quicker than the memory.

'I've made my decision. You'll have another Sentinel. Try to bring him back alive this time.'

Zarifah nodded her head weakly. 'I trust I'll be well paid.'

'Only if you do your job well.' Nigil smirked. He turned his attention to the holographic screen and the numbers that he scrolled down.

Leaving Nigil's office, Zarifah felt heavy with the smell of rotting flesh of guilt from the harvest. She completed the evening routine by visiting Ink Master to have the single flower tattooed on her skin; the line of flowers around her waist more and more like a growing vine, snaking around slowly, reaching out to where it had begun.

'Hear you had some trouble with katners,' said Ink Master over the hum of the machine.

'Hopefully Torin will be out before the end of the week when I go back to Kade's House.'

'You want to go back?'

'It's risky.' The quickest way for her belt to be finished was at Kade's House. There was nothing worth harvesting here with the type of patrons Nigil was encouraging to come. *I'll get more flowers.*

'I feel like I say the same thing to you over and over. Be careful, Zarifah.' He finished the small tattoo. 'Done.'

'I'll be fine.' Zarifah left, kissing him playfully on the cheek. She wasn't about to share her fears with the Ink Master. Navigating through the empty corridors, Zarifah went to the isolation area. Electric lights flashed a red warning as she approached the locked doors and pressed the intercom.

'Yes?' said a scratchy voice.

'Here to check on Torin.'

'You can't, he's isolated.'

'I just want to speak to him.' Zarifah buzzed the intercom repeatedly when there was no answer.

'I'm the Soul Dancer. I have to check on him.'

Eventually the door clicked open and she walked into the white sterile area. She waited, while she remembered the layout of the area, having spent a few times here after picking up a parasite when scavenging last year.

'This way,' said a short man dressed in white scrubs. Zarifah followed him down a small corridor to a room on the right.

Torin sat on a basic bed in what looked more like a prison cell than a room where a person would receive medical help. He smiled when he saw Zarifah through the window.

The short man pointed to an intercom by the window before leaving.

Zarifah looked back at Torin. Her breath caught in her lungs. *Her help him heal.* 'You Okay?' Her voice was distorted through the old intercom.

'Been better.' His voice strained with pain. He wore only white loose pants. A white bandage on his shoulder had a shadow of red showing through.

'So far I have lost count of how many injections I've had. Hopefully I will be out soon.' He slipped off the bed and gasped, falling back, panting with agony.

Zarifah leant forward. *If only I could help him.* She wished the glass wasn't there separating them. *If only I could hold him.*

Feel his skin under my fingers. Have him out here with me doing Her's work.

Torin pushed himself onto his feet and swayed a little before he found his balance. He stumbled over to the window.

Zarifah held up her hand. She blinked back the tears in her eyes. It hurt seeing him like this.

'Get better and hurry up about it.' She didn't mean the words to be so harsh.

He pressed his hand over hers on the other side of the glass. She wanted him be on her side, helping, and she wanted him to be there when they challenged Nigil, and took over. *He'll support me.* And she was in need of support for the plan to work. The weight of what was to come weighed heavily on her shoulders. Even now, palm on the glass, looking into his eyes, it wasn't enough.

'Be careful. I hate to think what could happen.'

'You take care in here. I hate to think what could happen if you're not out and keeping an eye on Hayal.' Zarifah forced herself to smile, to show that she was brave and to ignore the turmoil of fear that was bubbling inside of her. She walked away. *I miss him.*

Wandering down the corridors alone, she decided to see if she could sneak into the Alchemist's room.

'Is The Collector in?' Zarifah asked the Sentinel at Nigil's office.

'No.' He shifted his stance to fully block the door.

'Why are you here then?' She saw a softness in his brown eyes.

He shrugged. 'Orders.'

'Is he coming back?'

The Sentinel shook his head. *Good.* Zarifah stepped closer. 'Tell me your name?'

'Kereta.' The crystal around his neck, a ball shape, pulsed a soft orange light of his trapped soul. She could sense the softness in him, the gentleness. *He did well to survive the soul split.*

'Well then it's not that bad, some positives.' She leaned close to him. 'Like me.'

Running her hand over his chest, shivers of energy rippled from her touch. He was young, naive and now Zarifah had a new toy to mould as she liked. The plan of the future pulsing in time with her actions.

'How about you let me in?'

'Been told not to let anyone in.' His voice edged with doubt.

'Yeah, but you weren't told specifically not to let me in, were you?'

His forehead wrinkled with doubt. 'No, but that's—'

'No one except you and me will know. See how easy it is to help people down here and make friends. But you see you can only do this little favour for me, otherwise it won't be special between us.'

He nodded as if intoxicated by her words and presence.

Kereta stepped aside and Zarifah quickly swiped the copied chip of Nigil's as she distracted the Sentinel with a light kiss on his cheek. Then she walked into the dark office. Taking a deep breath, she stood allowing her eyes to adjust to the glow of an orange light, before walking through to the back rooms.

Oren worked at the bench.

'Working late?'

The Alchemist jumped in surprise. His eyes focussed slowly on Zarifah. 'You've set me some big tasks,' said the Alchemist.

'I have more crystals to be emptied,' said Zarifah.

'You've been busy too.' He took the crystals and placed one in the metal box, closed the lid and began punching a sequence of buttons.

'I want a machine like that one but smaller. Can you arrange that for me?'

'No, it would be too risky giving you a machine. Nigil's bound to find out and that will be the end of my life. Even though it sucks, for some damned reason I want to keep living it.'

'It's too risky me coming here so often. Nigil's more likely to find out this way. Each night I will potentially have two crystals to empty and I can't come here each night.'

'Pity.' Oren changed over the crystals.

'So can you?'

'Yeah, but I don't know that's going to be a good idea.' Doubt clouded his eyes.

'I will still be coming here, to check on your progress in reversing the splitting of the soul.' Zarifah smiled sweetly, trying to influence him. 'Anyway, you would tire of me if I saw you every night.'

'Doubt it.' He handed her back the two crystals and two phials of clear liquid.

'Remember that if I was in charge, then you would be free from this room.' She slipped the crystals and phials in her bra.

'But you aren't in charge.'

'Yeah, but I will be. So whose side do you want to be on? Mine or Nigil's?' She held out her hand to stop him from touching her body, giving him a stern look.

He paused as if thinking about his options, his mind working hard to decide. 'Yours.'

'Good then when I've come to power, you can have your motivation then,' said Zarifah. 'Consider it motivation.' She pushed him away from her not wanting to touch him a minute longer. 'How long to make me the machine?'

'I want…'

'Only if you come through with my request.' Zarifah fluttered her eyelashes. *And then I'll be in charge and I won't have to give myself as payment.*

'Two days.'

'That quick?' She picked up an empty crystal and turned it over in her hand.

'The Collector allows us to have the equipment we need, more or less. It's not hard to get what we need down here, in terms of electronics and metal.'

'Glad to hear Nigil is generous about something. Two days, then,' said Zarifah as she left. It was a lot of time, but it was progress. Her mind shifted thought options. *Now I just need to make sure I'm the Collector.*

18

Zarifah bowed at the feet of Her. The etheric hands of Her rested on Zarifah's head sending a gentle vibration though her form.

Soon my dear, I will be reunited to the source and pulse with the Earth once more. Then we can meet in the flesh once I have been reincarnated as the true goddess of the Earth. Then we can heal the lands and our disciples will return to their peaceful power.

Zarifah answered, *It will be a blessed day*. Excitement pulsed through her body. She noticed Her's form was even more transparent. *Thank you for the lesson*. New knowledge filled her mind adding a peaceful vibration to her essence.

Go now. Continue this good work.

Zarifah's awareness slipped away from the astral plane and settled back in her body. She opened her eyes, blinking to refocus them. Worry blurred the edges of her mind. Her won't last much longer. She stretched out her legs from underneath her; blood flowed to the starved muscles with a pulsing ache. It had been a long session. Her mind was getting more accustomed to slipping off the Astral plane and she hadn't needed to rely on incense to help.

A click at her door caused Zarifah's back to stiffen.

Nigil stood in the doorway. He wore a dark green chequered suit and the smell of soap wafted from him. 'Come,' Nigil commanded.

That was close. Zarifah got up and followed him. *Please Her not another poor child.* But they remained on the dormitory level. Faint screams ahead confirmed they were going to visit Malkia. Zarifah braced herself and pushed down her own torment of remembering the split of her own soul as they walked into the room. Hayal bent over the young dancer, sponging her forehead.

'Go with the others to scavenge,' said Nigil he stood by the bed. Malkia strained against the straps. Hayal reluctantly left.

'Let me go,' she moaned.

Zarifah pursed her lips tight. *It's her soul that wants to be free.* Her own trapped soul pulsed in a panicked rhythm.

'Can she integrate?' asked Nigil.

Zarifah knelt next to the bed. 'Look at me, Malkia.' She tried to coax the girl to forget about the separation.

'Why? So you can burn me,' said the girl, Her eyes opened in a fiery flash of blue, long enough for Zarifah to know. Besides, it was obvious from the screaming that the integration hadn't occurred and the fire in the girl's eyes confirmed that it never would. Yet Zarifah lingered. *What went wrong?* Could she fix the girl with the emotions she would collect or could she lie to Nigil just to keep the girl alive?

'Well?' Nigil demanded. The tone in his voice broke any hope Zarifah had for Malkia. She couldn't even bring herself to lie; the girl was too far gone.

Zarifah stood shaking her head. 'No, there's too much fire in her soul. She will not integrate.' Tears welled in Zarifah's eyes. *If only I could've saved her.*

'What a waste.' He pulled out a glass phial and began to fill a syringe. 'To help her sleep.'

Zarifah breathed a sigh of relief that he wasn't going to end Malkia's life. But she couldn't help think it might have been a welcome release if he would.

A Sentinel knocked at the door. 'Collector, a pod is requesting permission to speak to you.'

Zarifah stayed with Malkia until she settled. The drugs worked quickly. *If only I could've stopped this.* She clenched her jaw. *I will. I just have to work out how to remove Nigil.* The goddess wanted him dead, but Zarifah didn't see why. There was enough death down here and she didn't want to add to it.

'Collector wants you,' said the Sentinel. His voice broke her thoughts and she stood up, body stiff.

'Of course.' She felt like a dog on a very short leash.

She walked into the room and froze at the sight of a boy of about ten standing in shabby clothes and smelling of fear. She looked into his big brown eyes with golden flecks and looked deep into his soul.

'Is he skilled?' asked Nigil.

'Yeah.' Zarifah glanced at the door behind Nigil's desk. Would Oren have the machine ready? The plan was slowly taking shape. Re-joining the souls was the answer to their freedom.

'Take him in, they are waiting.' The Sentinel carried the boy through to the adjacent room. Zarifah braced herself for the screams, the new screams of betrayal, of realising you had just been separated from something you valued so much but hadn't realised you had such a precious gem inside of you. As usual her knees buckled from the sound and Nigil, cold as metal, stood smirking at her. 'It's not that bad.'

Bastard. An acidic taste filled her mouth.

The Sentinel came out a few minutes later. The boy was unconscious in the Sentinel's arms, his small frame twitched involuntary. 'Take the boy and leave him in Hayal's care. She likes children.'

Zarifah turned to leave.

'Not so quickly.' He beckoned her to him with a long finger as if it was pulling that invisible leash towards him. Zarifah hesitated. Her mind screamed no.

A knock on the door interrupted them. Zarifah exhaled with relief.

'Enter.' He frowned.

A Sentinel walked in. 'They're here.'

'Get the girl,' said Nigil and stood from his chair.

Two male Regulators and one female walked into the room. A sucking sensation moved over Zarifah's body as they tasted her emotions.

'You have a collection for us?' said the female.

'Failed the integration,' said Nigil.

'A black mark for the House. Though it is only your second for the year,' said the female.

'We do take the integration process seriously,' said Nigil.

'Sure, and we take the emotions you harvest, so we want as much emotion as possible rather than you handing back failed dancers. Who's your Soul Dancer?' Nigil pointed to Zarifah, who bowed her head.

'You trained the girl.'

Zarifah nodded.

'And why can't she harvest?'

Zarifah felt the putrid smell of guilt being sucked from her. She tried to hold herself apart and keep her balance. 'She showed potential. She could dance, but her soul fought the integration.' Her head pounded

'But why?'

'Her skill diminished and her soul fought. I don't know why.' Zarifah guessed why. The knowledge of the Soul Dancers were failing, just like Her in the Astral plane. The skill was weaker in the next generation, especially without training. But she wasn't about to tell them this. She wanted the Regulators to fail.

'We will take her and complete experiments.' The female's voice was flat and cold.

'Maybe it's time this House had a new Soul Dancer.'

'She is our best,' interrupted Nigil.

'Then why are we here?'

Zarifah lowered her eyes nervously. She needed to be Soul

Dancer to do Her's work. *Or do I? If I'm The Collector…* She lifted her eyes to Nigil.

'It's the girl's fault. She doesn't have the skill,' said Nigil.

Kereta carried the unconscious girl into the room. *No please don't take her.* But Zarifah didn't move. The girl was lost and she had failed. *Think of the plan.* Her mouth went dry as they took her away.

'This is to be your last failed integration,' advised the Regulator. The warning sent Zarifah's nerves fluttering in her stomach. She stood waiting for instruction from Nigil.

'Go, the Regulators have sucked away any desires I had.' Nigil pushed her away and swivelled his chair around to stare at the concrete wall. 'Maybe they're right, you might be the best Soul Dancer I have seen, but maybe I should give the title to someone else.'

The words prickled her skin as Zarifah left the room, but for once all she could think about was how she could get his position. *Then I'll make changes.*

***

'They've taken her,' sobbed Hayal in Zarifah's room.

Zarifah placed a comforting arm around Hayal. The new boy, O'yal, stood outside nervously playing with the cord on his black harem pants.

'You always knew that they would.'

'Yeah, but… what hope have we got down here?'

'Hayal, pull yourself together. You're going to have to do

the main harvest tomorrow night when I'm over at the Angel House.' That idea in part cheered her up.

'Torin won't be out of isolation?' She wiped her eyes.

'Hopefully he will, but he won't be able to dance, so it's up to you.' Zarifah felt a little nervous about giving up her position after the suggestion the Regulators had made. The girl's sobs subsided.

'Go and pray to Her, and tell O'yal a story about Her. Can't have you blubbering around when there's Her's work to do.'

'I'm starting to think you trust me, Zarifah,' said Hayal wiping away her tears.

'Go and make sure you're ready for tomorrow night.' Zarifah pushed the girl out of her room.

'Do you ever think that we tell the younglings too much about Her, so when they dance the first time they are more likely to fight the integration process,' said Hayal quietly so the Sentinel who had been placed outside couldn't hear.

'Shh, no.' She closed the door. Two empty crystals were hidden in her room ready to be filled at the Angel House.

A few minutes later a gentle tap at her door forced her out of bed. She trudged over to open the door.

'What are you doing here?' asked Zarifah shocked as Oren walked in.

'You hadn't visited.' The door slid shut and he wrapped his arms around her.

Zarifah squirmed out of his embrace. 'It's too risky.' *I don't need a cocky Alchemist ruining my plans.* 'And I thought you couldn't leave the rooms?'

'Let's say you inspired me, and Nigil's drunk, with a little extra help from something I gave him.' The Alchemist smiled proudly before trying to kiss her again.

'Stop it,' said Zarifah firmly. 'What did you do to the Sentinel?'

'Sleeping too.'

Zarifah rolled her eyes. *Her help us.* 'Nigil better not realise.'

'Thought you'd be wanting to get your hands on this.'

Oren held up a metal box that fitted easily into his hand. Zarifah smiled, temporarily forgetting the man's indiscretions.

'It's beautiful,' said Zarifah.

'Yeah well, it's not perfect, but it will do the job. You have to recharge the batteries. The batteries will only do one extraction, if that. I sacrificed the batteries for the size…'

Zarifah planted a kiss on the man's cheek. An empty kiss, one that was very different to the kisses she now gave Torin.

'Well I'll have some more of that,' he said but Zarifah pushed him away.

'Remember I have had to do this for a living, it means nothing to me.' Zarifah opened a flap on the side of the box to reveal a small panel of buttons.

'I hid the electronics so that to most people it would look like a simple box.'

'Do you have something to test it with?' said Oren.

'Thought you would?' Zarifah shook her head.

'I expect something a little more, intimate tonight?' The Alchemist held up a crystal pulsing with a faint orange light.

'You really have outdone yourself,' said Zarifah.

'Yes, well like I said I have motivation.' He looked hungrily at Zarifah.

'Can I keep the crystal?' She pressed the crystal into the box. It clicked into place.

'No, have to take it back.'

'Nothing special then.'

'But it's not full of darkness.'

Zarifah shook her head. She could smell the freshness of curiosity.

'Keep the crystal then but I want something in return.' Oren stepped towards Zarifah. She stepped away from him and plugged in the metal box and closed the lid. The machine hummed for a few minutes then a small green light flashed. She opened the box, taking out the phial, she could smell the curiosity.

'Should the crystal be sterilised?'

'Take out the phial and then press here for the cleaning cycle.' His hands brushed against hers.

Zarifah had learnt that nothing was for free in this world. But there was no way she was going to give any intimate favours to Oren. 'Later. It will be worth the wait.'

'Let's drink the phial,' said Oren.

'That's not wise,' said Zarifah trying to suppress the new wave of curiosity rising from within. She had tried this with happiness and it was something more exciting than she could've ever imagined.

'I thought you wouldn't mind experimenting?' said the Alchemist.

'No.' Zarifah held firm. 'And I'm beginning to think that

you don't trust me, which makes me think you're no use to me anymore.' She narrowed her eyes at him.

'That's not true.'

'Then prove it. Get me whatever drug you gave the Sentinel.' She lifted her chin at him.

'I need more motivation than that.' Oren looked smug.

'How about I go tell Nigil that you've been stealing emotions, or that you came here to fuck me?'

'You wouldn't dare.' Oren's forehead wrinkled.

'Why not? You're not willing to help me.' She lowered her voice. 'You're reluctant to do Her's work.'

'How do I know it would be worth waiting?'

'Do you want to keep living like this?'

Oren shook his head.

'Good. Now go and do what I've asked you.' Zarifah opened the door and pushed him out. The Sentinel still slept. *Doing whatever I need to bring Her back is much harder than I thought.*

19

'Ready?' Nigil looked closely at Zarifah as they stood in the loading area. For the performance at the Angel House tonight she had chosen a skirt of polyester, cut into strips, which revealed her white legs between the black pieces. The belt was trimmed with grey metal she had scavenged and formed into circles of flowers. They were great at hiding things like crystals. Three empty crystals hid in her belt waiting to be filled. Black polyester material covered her breasts. Smaller chains of metal hung around her chest, mirroring the slightest movement of her body and drawing attention. Her hair was braided into one long plait that fell down the centre of her back. Scars of old and new were revealed and her back looked like a large cat had come along and used it as a scratching mat.

'You won't need these,' said Nigil unclipping the empty collection crystals from around her neck as if it pained him to release such objects from her. 'Shame, numbers are improving and you go off for one night, Torin can't dance and once again I have to rely on Hayal. This is not good for business.'

'You could've said no to Kade.' Zarifah met his grey eyes defiantly.

'Come back in good condition this time.' He looked at the Sentinel standing next to Zarifah. 'Kereta, you keep her alive, then yourself.'

In the shuttle Zarifah looked out onto the wastelands of Earth and Her's cry of despair trundled through her body. Piles of rubbish helped to locate where Houses were, other shuttles ferried patrons from bigger ships orbiting above the atmosphere to Houses for a night of frivolity. Buildings of old stood like man-made monsters on sentinel duty ready to fall on whoever shook their foundations. They had been stripped of any useful material years ago.

'Just a sea of grey and black,' said Kereta. 'Makes our warrens look like paradise.'

'So many shades of dullness,' said the pilot.

'How do you navigate through such bleakness?' asked Zarifah. This time she didn't feel so sick from the movement of the shuttle.

'The only way, especially if the grey clouds of pollution come in low,' said the pilot as he tapped the electronics on the console in front of him. As if guiding a bee to land, the shuttle connected to the landing gear of Kade's House.

'My dear, welcome back, I am going to enjoy these regular meetings,' said Kade. 'Come, you're late and will have to dance shortly.'

Zarifah followed Kade the short distance to the stage.

'You're up now,' said The Presenter. He strode past them and out onto the stage to introduce Zarifah and prepare the crowd.

The electric flutes played out the melody and Zarifah prepared for her harvest. The bright stage lights concealed the audience in darkness. She had to rely on her sense of smell to find an emotion worth harvesting.

Her body worked automatically, hips snapped in time with the sharp notes of the flutes, flowing arms with the silences as the notes rippled throughout the spaces around the bar. Drawing out the emotions deliberately from un-expecting patrons, she hunted for a source that would be strong enough to fill the crystals around her neck and those hidden in her belt.

She found her patron quickly. A Breather, the markings on the side of the neck light—this one was a male—sat at one of the tables. *A gift from Senara?* But it wasn't happiness that she smelt.

Zarifah approached the Breather and began tempting his emotion out. *It will do.* She longed for happiness, instead detected the freshness of curiosity.

Zarifah danced seductively, directing the curiosity towards the collecting crystals around her neck until they were full, then began moving the emotion to the hidden crystals in her belt, but there wasn't enough emotion to fill them and she was forced to sever the connection with the Breather before they were full. She left the stage, annoyed that she hadn't been able to fully fill the crystals around her waist.

Kade met her side stage. 'Let's see what you've harvested

for me.' He unclipped the two crystals and handed them to an Alchemist wearing a black coat full of holes and burns.

Zarifah shifted nervously while waiting to see how many flowers she'd be given tonight.

The Alchemist returned, his face unreadable. 'Curiosity. Good quality.'

'The value?'

'Two.' Kade nodded and the Alchemist left.

That's good. Slowly but surely her belt would soon be completed. *Ten and a half to go.* She turned to leave.

'Not so fast. You've been requested.'

Zarifah's shoulders squared. *Senara?*

'There's another client for you,' said Kade.

'Flann, take her to the room.' The wiry man ushered Zarifah away.

'Remember to please,' said Kade as she left.

'Of course.' Zarifah followed him. *Senara isn't too hard to please.* Her pulse quickened to a double time beat the closer she came to the private room.

'Your room,' said Flann as he unlocked the door using the push-button panel and Zarifah stepped into the darkened room.

She was alone and the decoration was the same as last time. Her fingers fidgeted around her waist, caught between desire to take the crystals out or not to because she didn't know who was going to be in her room tonight. *It might not be Senara.*

The door slid open and a tall figure walked in. The sucking sensation rippled over Zarifah.

'My favourite, I can always rely on Kade to deliver what I want.' Senara stepped over to Zarifah and ran her finger down the side of her face.

Zarifah closed her eyes and braced herself. *This isn't what I want.* But then having a Regulator on her side could mean the difference of her plan working or not.

'Hmmm, the softness of faint curiosity, fresh and alive,' said Senara as she smelled around Zarifah's neck. 'Give me more.'

'It doesn't work that way,' said Zarifah. 'I can't turn on my emotions.'

'It hasn't been a problem before, so let's get started. I plan to feed well tonight, it is just a shame that you have to be enslaved, means I have to be patient and you work twice as hard to release that emotion of yours.'

'You could release me?' said Zarifah.

'Yeah if I wanted to be hanged and quartered, the Emotionless do that still you know. Barbaric act of our past human lives.' She kissed Zarifah and sucked out the hint of curiosity left over from the harvest.

'Drink?' asked Zarifah when she was finally released from Senara's strong lips. She felt disorientated from the kiss.

'You're the only one I am drinking tonight. I am beginning to think that you are holding back deliberately and that I will have to get rough with you.' And she kissed Zarifah again, lightly sending shivers along the dancer's body.

'Now that's better.' Senara continued feeding on any emotion Zarifah produced. Once again Zarifah surrendered, allowing herself to be cleansed of emotions that she no longer cared for. Clothing slipped away as Senara urged her to give more. It seemed to go on for hours but eventually Senara fell back on the cushions breathing shallow and hard.

They lay next to each other with arms and legs tangled in their nakedness.

'I wish my body would hold the emotions longer,' said Senara as she traced her finger around the nearly finished tattoo. 'Though I do enjoy exploring your body, even though I know it well, the different emotions you release each time make me want more.'

Zarifah gave a fake smile, and reminded herself why she was really here; because Nigil was failing at running his House. And because Senara could help her when she became The Collector of the Wolf House.

'I do enjoy our time together,' said Zarifah, playing along.

Senara continued to move her hands lightly over Zarifah's body as they lay on their sides, naked bodies facing each other, kissing the other, one wanting more, the other wanting less.

'Kade will be after my flesh if I don't please you well because of the impure harvest,' said Zarifah hoping this session would soon end. All she wanted now was to learn how many tattoos she had earned with Senara and then leave.

'As for pleasing me, let's see what else I can feed from you before making my decision.' Senara leant over and began kissing the dancer again. Zarifah was tired and there wasn't much emotion for Senara to take. The woman soon pulled back in frustration.

Zarifah bit her lip to stop herself from apologising and

hoped that she had pleased the woman enough. She kept her head down while Senara dressed.

'I will tell Kade you were okay tonight, just okay.' Senara threw a money chip on the floor in front of Zarifah.

'Thank you and may—'

'Don't you dare try and bless me with Her. Look at me. I have no emotions, I feed off of other humans. This is what Her has created.' Senara punched the panel to open the door and left. Zarifah dressed quickly, hiding the chip under the material around her waist and planned to use the credit to buy some flowers for her tattoo from Nigil. *If he let's me.*

20

'I hear that you all survived last night,' said Nigil. He had summoned her to his office before the scavenging began for the day.

'How did Hayal perform last night?' Zarifah suppressed a yawn.

'Well enough.'

'A chip full of money to transfer into flowers,' said Zarifah. Nigil took the chip and plugged it into the console, releasing a whistle.

He whistled. 'Who did you perform for?' he asked.

'Just another low life, apparently one with money.' He was curious and she didn't need confirmation from the faint smell of citrus emanating from him. Zarifah tried to lean over to see how much money was on the chip.

'I'll give you a flower,' said Nigil.

'There's enough money for more, five at least,' said Zarifah feeling the heat of resentment rising from deep within.

'Ahh, but I can't afford to have you running around free, at least not until I have secured an end to lending you to Kade.' His grin turned Zarifah's stomach as hope faded she would ever be able to finish the belt and gain her freedom.

'It's your poor management that has caused you to have to loan me to Kade,' said Zarifah. Anger burned in her throat and the words came out before she could stop them.

'You're out of line.' Nigil moved from behind the table towards Zarifah.

'I'm owed flowers,' said Zarifah trying to make her voice sound firm in a battle of words she wouldn't win.

'What did you do?' he asked softly as if he was stalking prey and wanting to coax her closer into false hope.

'Nothing that I haven't already done with you.' Zarifah kept her hands locked in front of her belly to stop herself from fidgeting as he approached.

'But I wouldn't give you that amount of money.'

'That's because you don't have that amount to give.'

'Which is why I'm going to keep it, and you'll get no flowers.'

'Not even one?'

'No. Now leave before I decide to get my whip out,' said Nigil, his tone calm and calculating.

Zarifah turned to leave and got as far as the door before Nigil spoke again.

'Another new dancer tonight, the boy is doing well. Don't neglect your dancers, or I will be shipping you away next.'

Zarifah navigated through the levels of the House, frustration simmered in her stomach. She'd lost the chip. No flowers and the thought of choosing another young dancer to begin harvesting tonight made her gut twist and knot.

'The Soul Dancer has returned,' said Torin. He held his shoulder stiffly as he walked towards her.

'You've been released.' Zarifah tentatively kissed him on the lips. A friendly kiss, not at all like the one she wanted to give him.

'Finally.' They continued walking through the corridors towards Zarifah's room.

'When can you dance again?' Zarifah pressed the panel to open the door to her room.

'Maybe in a week. The wounds are deep and the cream can't penetrate that far according to the tech.' They walked into her room and Torin went straight to the bed, groaning in pain as he sat, his muscular body awkwardly leaning forward out of the smaller alcove.

'No Medic?'

'Zarifah, I don't think Nigil has got any money and since when did he bother to bring them in, only when there's a risk of an infection spreading and he risks losing a number of his dancers at once.

'That's not good for us,' said Zarifah. She clenched her jaw.

'So what else did you get from the Angel House? Good to know that everyone came back alive and without infections.'

Zarifah took a deep breath and sat cross-legged in front of Torin, told him about Senara.

'I don't like you with her,' said Torin.

Zarifah gazed as his face. Forgetting about Senara, and Nigil, as she looked into his blue eyes. 'I've missed you.'

Torin leaned forward and kissed her. Zarifah breathed in the intoxicating smell of happiness and wanted more.

'I have something we can use.' Standing, Zarifah went to one of the hidden compartments in her room and pulled out the crystals and began to systematically transfer the emotions they contained in the phials. They weren't full but she hoped it would be enough to satisfy her for a while.

'You really are taking this seriously and risking a lot.' He sighed heavily. 'How about you just come back here.'

'In the name of Her, I have to take restoring the old teachings back to power seriously.' She clipped shut the box and it hummed, emptying the crystal. She cleaned it and repeated the process.

'Have you thought what will happen if you failed?'

'There would be someone here to take over.' She looked over her shoulder. Torin's blue eyes widened.

'But what if I can't?'

'You can.' Zarifah put away the box and crystals, and took two phials of happiness with her to the bed. 'I thought that you believed in Her, and that failure wasn't an option. Are you planning on giving up, Torin?'

'No, I just had to be sure you were determined and not just flitting around trying to make yourself more powerful.' He kissed her gently. He opened his hand.

'I found it scavenging a while back, always hard to trade with even though they are a priceless find.' A small crystal, pulsing with some emotion, lay on his palm.

'Why didn't you give this to me sooner?' asked Zarifah as

she picked up the crystal and held it to the poor light that illuminated her room.

'You had no way of using it, besides I was out of pills and needed something to trade. But as you know trade isn't happening right now.'

'Thanks,' said Zarifah as she concealed the crystal for later and handed him a phial. 'Like before only weaker.'

'I don't know that we should be doing this again,' said Torin.

Zarifah consumed the liquid in one big sip.

'We should be keeping such valuable emotion for trade. You don't know what equipment you might need in the future. Besides you can't keep sleeping with everyone, at least not misusing Her's teachings.' He turned the phial between his fingers.

His words flamed a sore spot within in her. 'I'm no more of a whore than you are. I'm not harming anyone. This helps to raise us higher and will help us do Her's work.' Zarifah leaned into his body and slid her hand down his face.

'This is a valuable commodity down here. We shouldn't be wasting it on us.' He held her hand, stopping its caress over his face.

'We have to test our products first. This is what we are doing. Then we can trade with more experience, rather than in ignorance,' said Zarifah.

Torin hesitated. Then drank.

Zarifah kissed him, hard. Knocking him back on the bed. He pushed back, lips on hers, as they joined more than their physical bodies, intertwining with the happiness transforming the energy into ecstasy and then holding themselves there, suspended in the heights of euphoria they looked at each other before tumbling down, in a crashing spiral back down to the reality of their dark lives.

'We have to go and practise,' said Torin dreamily. He traced his fingers over her bare belly.

'Told you it was worth testing.' She kissed him lightly before standing and dressing.

'But no more, Zarifah. Not with the happiness, it changes you too much.' He sat up, groaning in pain. Blood had begun to stain through the bandages.

'Besides we don't need it.'

Zarifah helped him to dress. 'You don't want to feel happiness?' asked Zarifah.

'No, it's just not right for us to be using the collected emotion like this. It isn't our emotion. Let's try to make our own happiness.'

'It's not right for us to have part of our soul split and contained in this crystal. How can we make any such joy when our souls are imprisoned? Nothing wrong with having a little help.' She kissed him playfully on the cheek. 'There isn't enough love between us to ever produce happiness, not in a hell hole like this.'

'Don't become reckless Zarifah, I would miss you if something were to happen.' He tried to embrace her but she moved away, the spicy smell between them fading as she walked to the door.

'Let's go and practise and see who's ready to dance for the first time tonight.' Torin followed her through the falsely lit corridors to the practice room. Other dancers were there already warming up.

'Younglings come here and dance for us,' said Zarifah clapping her hands. With recorded music playing, the young girls and boys danced in front of Zarifah and Torin. O'yal was awkward after only a few lessons but he was learning quickly. Etana was moving more fluidly now, but she wasn't ready, and Zarifah would hold her back as long as possible. She didn't want the girl to go through the first time where she betrayed the teachings of Her. Zarifah wanted her to be one of the first who could use the dancing to honour Her.

'That girl, Kardelen,' said Hayal as she slipped between Zarifah and Torin, putting her long white arms over their shoulders. Hayal was probably right; the girl she had pointed to showed the most promise of the group. It wasn't like she had a choice tonight; someone had to dance and these younglings weren't up to the standard she wanted.

'How are you two lovebirds going? Who would've thought that love could be found down here?' She winked at Torin who returned a cold stare.

'You know love isn't something us dancers find down here.' *I have to be more careful.*

'Hayal, go and work on the stomach rolls with the younglings until they can control their bodies.'

Hayal pulled a face but she did as instructed. Zarifah narrowed her eyes as the younger dancer walked away.

'I'm sick of bringing in a harvest for someone else,' said Torin quietly to Zarifah.

'Which is why I am going to give you a crystal. You're right, it's time we began to make our own stock.'

'There's no point in having our own stock if we drink it,' said Torin. 'But I'm not sure I can dance yet.'

'I'll help you. Once I have made my selection for the night, you and Hayal move around and you fill the crystals that I give you.'

'Risky.'

'It will work.'

'It's better. I don't want to lose you.' He brushed a finger along her bare arm as they stood close together.

Spiciness wafted between them. 'You won't.'

21

Nigil unclipped the crystals around Zarifah's neck and handed them to Oren. He held her hands tightly to stop them shaking. This wasn't the first time she had trouble with patrons, but the threat to her was real and she trembled with the fear of what could've happened. *Lucky a Sentinel stepped in.* Zarifah touched the side of her cheek. Her skin tingled where the patron had hit her. She remembered his eyes, the evil intent that shone back at her. A cold shiver prickled her skin, stirring the unpleasant memories within her of past mishaps.

'Here take this,' said Nigil his voice compassionless. He handed her two yellow pills. Without hesitation she swallowed them. She hated standing vulnerable like this in front of Nigil.

'Pure,' said Oren. 'Worth five.' Before leaving he tried to make eye contact with Zarifah but she kept her eyes averted as anger roiled through her that he would be so bold.

'I'll give you three flowers.'

Zarifah tried to speak but her voice wouldn't work, instead tears formed which were hard to suppress as she began to berate herself for such weakness. Her mind calculated how many flowers were left. *Seven and a half blue forget-me-nots.*

'I can't have you being free too soon.'

'That's unfair,' she whispered her voice barely audible.

'Everything is unfair down here.' His soul crystal flared with a red glow.

He is right.

'Go rest.'

Zarifah's legs barely held her upright as she walked back to her room. She didn't have the strength to go and see the tattooist. Three more flowers could wait, the problem now was that Nigil probably wouldn't allow her to complete her belt no matter how pure the emotion she harvested.

Opening the door to her room, she felt as if her time in this House was running out and soon she would be replaced, forgotten, her reign as Soul Dancer over before she could gain control. Before she even had a chance to restore Her.

She took out the crystals from her belt and put them aside to be emptied.

'You were lucky tonight,' said Torin as she handed over her crystal in the secrecy of Zarifah's room.

'What emotion?'

'Fear. I hadn't quite finished harvesting before the brute you were with starting making trouble. Should've been curiosity, but I'm sure it's tainted beyond use.'

'At least it's a start.' Zarifah placed the crystal next to the others.

'I've been praying to Her, just as you want me to.' He massaged his hands on her shoulders.

'I needed your help with the new dancer.' Zarifah eased into his touch.

'You don't need me for anything. You don't tell me your plans, and all I do is patch you up.'

'I do. I need you for this,' and she kissed him with a raw passion causing him to groan for more.

'Sometimes I wonder though,' said Torin but she ignored his words as she began to lift his shirt. Her mouth begged to taste the hints of spicy emotion but tonight there was nothing.

'Zarifah, not now, our bodies bleed too much,' said Torin removing her hands. 'We have plenty of time for that later.

'I think this will help us heal,' said Zarifah but she turned around and allowed him to apply the cream to her body.

'Lie down.' Zarifah cringed as she lay on her bed. Her body responded as he curled his around hers and together they slept, dreaming of a world where they were free.

The door slid open, almost silently, but the two continued sleeping. The sound of someone clearing their throat woke Zarifah. She opened her eyes, confused. Someone must have sneaked in silently while she slept. Only vaguely did she realise that Torin was next to her.

'What's this? A love nest?' Nigil stood over the bed.

Torin stood as quickly as his injured shoulder allowed, his muscular body towering above Nigil.

'This isn't allowed.' Nigil's voice thundered.

'Moment of weakness,' said Torin.

'It's nothing,' said Zarifah. A knot twisted in her stomach. *Nigil's going to kill him.* Her skin prickled and she sat up quickly on full alert.

'I really need to be working you much harder, Torin.' He placed his hand deliberately on his mending shoulder. Torin grimaced in pain.

'You don't have eyes for her anymore so why does it matter?' said Torin.

Nigil pressed harder. Torin moaned in agony.

'Nigil, let him go if you want him to be able to dance,' said Zarifah, her voice raspy.

'You answer to me, I own you. I own you both.'

'Yet you're not free yourself, how can you own us,' said Zarifah as she twirled the pendant at her neck. 'What's wrong with some comfort, some pleasure? We'll dance better because of it.'

Nigil slapped her hard. 'Things are changing, you'll both do well to remember that Her is dead and you use the skills for harvesting so that *we* can survive.'

'You get out. I'll have you whipped later.'

Torin left quickly, holding his shoulder.

'You, get cleaned, I have a client for you.'

'I want proper payment,' said Zarifah, her voice finding some strength.

'You'll do as I say if you want to remain alive.'

'You'll consider my request if you want me to harvest. The way I see it I may not be here long, so why bother keeping on with the harvesting.'

'I'll give you three flowers,' said Nigil his eyes narrowing with displeasure.

'Add them to my chip now.' Zarifah handed him her chip.

'You make sure you get me something worthy, or you'll get a whipping too, maybe a few hours alone with the katners as well. Kereta will escort you to the room upstairs.' Nigil left the room, taking a storm of strangled emotions with him.

Zarifah dressed in a full skirt, black fake silk with a golden wrap around her chest. Leaving her hair in numerous small black plaits. She stored the additional crystals in her belt. Nigil was double-crossing this patron by asking her to harvest his emotions, and she was just adding her finger to the pot making sure she would get something too.

She left the room. Kereta escorted her through the familiar corridors to the few rooms they had for the pleasure of high paying clients. She passed a few other dancers who were dressed warmly ready to go outside and scavenge.

'Nigil said to make you swallow.' Kereta handed her two pills, a nutrient and a pick-me-up, as well as her chip, now flashing two and half flowers to be added to her skin. *Of course.* He hadn't given her the payment promised. But then he had found her with Torin and Zarifah considered herself lucky to have even gotten this many flowers. Zarifah took them, wondering if Nigil was actually becoming soft, or if he wanted to ensure she would able to perform tonight.

'Enter,' a male voice answered.

Material adorned the room, colours of deep maroon and navy flowed down the walls hiding the boring, cold concrete walls and ceiling. Electric candles placed around the room added a soft light, enhancing the radiation of colour in the room. Music played quietly from a hidden recorder, a melody to help relax clients, not assist any harvest. Zarifah would have to work hard with her own pure skill to extract any emotion from this patron.

On big, square cushions, oriental in style, lay a man holding a small cup which he sipped from hungrily as Zarifah walked towards him. He patted the deep red cushion next to him and obediently she sat down.

She could smell the curiosity mixed with surprise. He wore no necklace and he produced concentrated emotions. His body was toned from hard physical work yet he was clean, wore the clothes of someone with money, not a trader working the black market of space.

Zarifah lifted the flask to re-fill his cup. She wanted his eyes to cloud over more, to help keep her safe, to help with a possible harvest. But he was only sipping, his lips on the cup and his eyes on her body.

She went to unbutton his white shirt, a soft fabric she hadn't felt for a long time, but he slapped her hands away with an unwarranted force. A little shaken, she took a deep breath to suppress her fears.

Slowly she began to unwind the gold cloth around her neck and he smiled as more skin was exposed. When her breasts were freed, he leant forward and kissed her nipples forcing her body to respond to his wet mouth and him to groan wanting more.

While he started exploring her body with mouth, Zarifah sent her senses to try and detect what emotions he had worth harvesting, but without the music, the lack of alcohol he'd consumed and no dancing, she was struggling to start the flow of emotion from him.

Her fingers worked in tandem with his lips, unbuttoning his shirt, his belt, his pants, feeling his body push his energy higher with hers. Begging him to want more of her. She wrapped her energy around his, pulsing gently for inlets into his. Like invisible fingers they found an opening and she entered him, while he entered her physically and together they gasped, one in pleasure the other in expectation.

Zarifah pulsed their energy back and forth, determined to achieve an extraction. Past the smells of rot and decay, fear. Following the tendril of faint cinnamon, she found the source deep within him, protected by the dark cloud of guilt.

Zarifah allowed herself to release gentle groans to act like feathers in the pool of happiness. Her notes of pleasure created a path towards herself and soon the happiness was flowing with a strong current towards her. The taste of the harvest on her lips made her mouth moist for more. She filled the crystals, hers first; this harvest was for herself.

When two of her crystals were full she began to fill the crystals around her neck. The current was weakening. She had taken too much, so that soon he would spiral downwards and there would be no pool of happiness for his soul to dive into, only a black cloud of guilt. Then he would notice the change, be angry, not knowing why, but most certainly she would be in trouble.

Ignoring the risk, she continued to encourage the flow, sealing off one of the crystals and then beginning on the last.

But the spicy scent had diminished. There was the distinct rank smell of fear.

The man had slowed, but there was room remaining in the crystal. She used her body to change positions with the man. Now she was on top and could keep her body pulsing, keep him occupied just a little longer while she completed the harvest.

He stopped groaning for more. Still the emotion flowed. Zarifah struggled to hold onto his energy to keep it high and just as she began to seal the last crystal, she realised how far she had gone.

With a final gasp his soul followed the last of his emotions, screaming at her to give them back, to give back the happiness she had stolen from him. With ruthlessness she showed his soul the path to the crystal and blindly he went down into the matrix of the crystal and held onto his fear. He moved in the crystal, sending a panic wave of charged energy towards her. She sealed the crystal and closed the pathway of return. His soul screamed in protest. Electric pulses pounded on the matrix, the crystal struggling to hold his soul. *Would the small matrix be able to keep such energy?*

She looked at the crystal with curiosity. There was a storm of energy inside. His body lay sweaty, exhausted, limp. Dead.

Bile rose to her mouth. Zarifah nearly opened up the crystal again. It would be difficult for her to do, but she looked at the lifeless body. Guilt cut at the insides of her stomach.

She had gone too far. The spicy aroma was now fighting with the stench of death in the air. Zarifah knew which scent would endure. The real cost ripped at her stomach. At least she had managed to gain payment on her chip before this harvest. The Ink Master wouldn't ask the questions, the number on the chip would be enough.

Nigil is going to kill me. Or at least be angry enough to blacken most of her body. Only four flowers were needed to decorate her waist. Zarifah wished she could harvest patience along with forgetfulness.

Zarifah lifted the crystal to her nose and breathed deeply. The spiciness hinted at the intoxicating happiness held in the matrix of the gems. Her tongue tingled in anticipation and her belly ached to have this essence inside, instinctively she began to try and coax the emotion back out for herself. She gasped as an electric shock sent out a warning. To drink the essence would help her to forget that she was nothing more than a whore, a slave, a rapist herself. The temptation was worth the electric buzz and so much more if she could.

Annoyed, she stumbled from the bed and rummaged through his clothes. Without thought she swallowed one of the tablets not even looking at the shape or colour. She slipped the remaining pills in her belt, and a small red gem under her tongue. A poor harvest from a supposed owner of a fleet. His electronic cards were too risky to take though she fingered their edges considering the wealth they could unlock for her. She replaced them carefully.

She covered her body with her dark robe, trying not to shake. Timing was now everything. She hoped Torin would be forgiving, but more importantly she prayed he'd be helpful in setting the scene.

Zarifah went to find Torin.

'Problem?' Kereta followed close behind.

'Don't you have to report back to Nigil?' said Zarifah annoyed that the Sentinel was going to keep following her.

'He'll expect you, so come this way.' He tried to grab Zarifah's arm.

'I've things to do.' Zarifah kept walking along the warren of corridors towards Torin's room.

'Which involve going to see Nigil, now.' This time he stopped Zarifah who lashed out and slapped the Sentinel. He kept his hold.

'I should haul your arse to the boss for that.' He gripped her tighter. 'Now come.'

'Fool. I killed him, I need to hide the body.'

'The Collector is going to have your skin for this.'

'Let me go to Torin. He'll know what to do.'

'No. I'll tie you up and drag you to him if I have to.' He kept hold of her arm. She pushed down the rising panic inside of her as the Sentinel forced her back towards Nigil's office. *Nigil's going to leave me to rot on the surface. I won't be able to help Her reincarnate. I've failed.* She stumbled next to the Sentinel. *I can bring him around. I just need to think of something.* The Sentinel pushed her into the office.

'Ah, my dear how did you go?' asked Nigil not even looking up from the console as he punched in a number of sequences and a series of symbols flashed on the screen. Zarifah stood wishing Her's voice would provide the words that needed to be spoken.

'Well?' Nigil looked up annoyed with the silence. 'You filled the crystals?'

Zarifah nodded.

'Excellent.' Nigil pressed a button on the desk and Oren came running into the room and took the crystals.

'I expect no less from you. But I am curious why so white?' His stare caused Zarifah to look to the ground as if in prayer. 'Speak, or I'll have you whipped.'

'You'll whip me anyway,' said Zarifah.

'Yes and I'll enjoy it. So the client I sent you wasn't happy?'

Zarifah shook her head. No matter how hard she willed herself she couldn't tell The Collector what had happened.

'Pure happiness in one extraction and the other is happiness tainted curiosity,' said Oren when he returned.

'Well, you must have managed to please him greatly. But what's got you worried?' Nigil paused and slammed his hand on the table. 'Tell me!'

'He's dead.'

'Fuck. The last thing I need is The Regulators to come and investigate again.' Nigil kicked the chair. 'How did you manage to kill such a strong man?'

'I took too much. I thought you wanted him dead.' Zarifah locked her knees to stop herself from running out of the room. For once in her time here she feared for her life. Besides she was openly lying to him.

'Harvested, not dead!' Nigil took a deep breath. 'Zarifah I think that I am going to sell you to the highest bidder.'

'I got you pure happiness, that is worth something.'

'And I have to find another captain to trade with.'

'You could always report he double-crossed you.'

'Then who would trust me?' He moved towards Zarifah and grabbed her throat. Nigil's eyes narrowed as he squeezed his fingers.

'You could establish yourself above other Houses here on Earth through the fear, you now own a fleet,' said Zarifah struggling to breathe but desperate for the words to save herself. Tears of fear spilled as she silently begged for her life.

'Zarifah, if you weren't so good at harvesting I would kill you myself. You're worth more to me here, and for once you may have a point worth acting on, which may just save your life. He released his grip. 'This time.'

Zarifah fell to the floor at Nigil's feet, gasping for air.

'Lock her in her room and take the body to the storage. And don't bother me with anything tonight, unless she tries to escape. I am going for a drink.'

Nigil walked out of the room while Kereta moved to help Zarifah from the floor.

'Please, take me to Torin, you owe me that,' she said hoarsely.

'I will, but I owe you nothing.' His eyes were soft as he spoke. 'I am loyal to Her.'

Walking towards the dormitories, Zarifah smelled the sharpness of the ceremonial herbs and instinctively followed the scent to the washrooms. She was glad that someone was brave enough to pray to Her, but it was too risky, the smell would bring a harsh whipping from Nigil and he was more than ready to release his anger on his dancers.

'Torin,' said Zarifah as she entered the rooms and found her friend cross-legged on the floor deep in meditation.

Zarifah stood in front of Torin wanting to slap him back to reality, but held back knowing such a fright could cause his soul to be caught between worlds. Besides she needed his help, and the after-taste of cinnamon left her wanting to experiment more with the new harvest with him.

The coolness in the air of the washroom hurt her throat as she leaned against the wall drumming her fingers on the railing. The metal echoes demanding attention. Torin's presence drifted back to his body.

'You can smell the herbs down the hall, anyone could've disturbed you,' said Zarifah as his blue eyes opened. 'What did Her say?'

'That you are doing a great job and that I am to trust you,' said Torin as he packed up the rug he'd sat on, and cleaned away the ashes.

'Good.' She was glad Her was pleased with her efforts. 'I have a job for us which we need to do now.'

'I don't know, Zarifah,' said Torin. He looked tired after the meditation.

'Here have one of these.' She pulled out some of the stolen pills. 'This one should do.'

Torin whistled and smiled as he swallowed one of the yellow pills.

'I don't even have to test that pill to know it was pure. Where did you get it?'

'From the man I killed tonight.' Determination thudded

through her body. *It's time to try this machine out whether it is ready or not.*

'So that's why your neck is bruised.' Concern shadowed his eyes and he rested this hand on her shoulder.

Zarifah pursed her lips together. *I can't tell him it was Nigil.* 'Come on, we have a body to experiment with.'

22

Zarifah fidgeted at the decorative chains hanging from her waist while Oren systematically strap the lifeless body on the table. Torin fidgeted by her side grating on her nerves.

'The machine's not ready.' Oren paused and looked at the others. 'This is not what I'd set the machine up for.'

'But it could work,' said Zarifah. She sat on the metal bench and crossed her legs.

'Yeah, it could work.' Oren began sticking pads attached to wires to the head and heart of the man with the machine.

'If it doesn't?' asked Torin.

'He's already dead,' said Zarifah. She shrugged. *We have to try. We can't keep living like this.*

'If we learn something about how the soul can be returned it will be a useful experiment. One that will bring us closer to reuniting the parts of our soul.'

'I don't know how you have managed this Zarifah, right in

front of Nigil.' Torin kissed her arm. Her skin buzzed from his soft touch, and her body ached for more. *Later.*

'Her's will.' She chewed her bottom lip. *If this works then I could end up the new Collector.*

'We will see if it was worth hurting my shoulder again by dragging this dead weight here.'

'Hurry up.' Zarifah glared at Oren who fumbled with the levers on the electrical box the wires were attached to.

'Gotta get the wiring correct, otherwise he'll be fried.'

'Good thing he's dead then,' said Zarifah. 'Here's the crystal with his soul.' She handed over the white cloudy rock.

Oren placed the crystal in a clasp near the head of the man. 'Ready?' Oren didn't wait for any comments and began pressing the control pad. The crystal responded straight away. The soft red light filled the matrix of the rock. Electricity pulsed between the crystal and the man, bringing the wires alive, creating a pathway for the imprisoned soul to flow out and return to the body.

The crystal began to fade in colour as the soul drained from its matrix and flowed through the wires.

'It's working,' said Torin, a look of hope in his eyes.

'No,' said Oren as the colour in the crystal returned. 'The crystal wants to keep the soul.'

'Can't you force it to release the soul?' asked Zarifah, clenching her fingers into a fist.

'It's too late now. I can't interfere with the electricity. It's a simple model, electricity is on or off and you keep your fingers out of the way.'

'Switch it off, make an adjustment, then try again.'

'Each time we try, the crystal's likely to gain strength. It will be harder to force it to release the soul. I could use electricity to try and shock the matrix open but the more energy I use the more likely that the soul will be fried and not released.' Oren rubbed his temples thinking.

'We've no choice. Do it.' She clenched her jaw. *This will work. Her make it work.*

'I don't know how much electricity to use.' Oren altered a few of the settings on the control panel. 'I don't know if this will work.'

'Try,' Zarifah demanded crossing her arms across her chest.

'Take two,' he said as the machine grumbled with a start. The crystal pulsed angrily with hues of red as if wanting to keep its prize. A flash of intense light followed by a sharp pop exploded into the room. Zarifah shielded her eyes, blinded temporarily. Adrenalin coursed through her body. A putrid odour filled the room.

'What's that smell?' Zarifah coughed.

'Did it work?' Torin pulled a cloth over his nose.

'No.' Oren turned a shade whiter. 'Burning soul.' Oren breathed shallow through his mouth. 'And crystal.' Oren picked up the crystal; now translucent black, its insides shattered.

'Crystal's useless,' said Oren. He removed the wires.

'You used too much electricity then?' said Torin. His eyebrows crossed and a shadow of anger clouded his face.

The Alchemist nodded. 'But now I know so much more, I think that this little experiment might have saved us weeks.'

'When will you be ready for another try?' asked Zarifah.

'Tomorrow,' said Oren. 'If you can get me someone else to experiment on…'

'Another body?' asked Torin. 'No way. We've gone too far as it is.'

'Well you boys are going to have to drag it back to the store room before Nigil realises it's gone.'

'This is going to cost you.' Torin groaned as he began to lift the man from the chair. The men struggled with the dead body.

'There's a way out back we can use,' said Oren. Sweat beaded on his forehead.

'Here let me help.' Zarifah stepped forward.

'Open the door ahead.'

Zarifah pushed hard on the heavy door. 'Where does this lead to?'

'To the rubbish chute.'

'You can't just put the body down the rubbish.' She leant on the door while the men carried the body through.

'Got a better idea?' asked Torin. 'You seem to be full of plans.'

Zarifah kept silent. *He's really annoyed at me.* For once she didn't have a better idea.

'Don't worry the katners will eat most of his flesh by tomorrow.' Oren puffed hard struggling to lift the body up to the chute.

'See, it will be all right.' Zarifah wanted to believe the words she said, but she wasn't sure. Hiding bodies wasn't what she wanted to be doing. *Sometimes there are mishaps which have to be dealt with.* She turned her head from the body as it was shoved down the chute. *Her forgive me.*

'I'm going to have a shower.' Torin brushed his hands together. He glared at Zarifah as he walked past and left. 'This better work out.'

'It will.' She willed him to come back but she didn't say anything. *Best he cools off a little.* Besides she wanted to have the night's payment added to her skin. 'I'll check on you later Oren.'

Oren nodded while whipping the sweat from his forehead onto his sleeve.

Zarifah walked to the Ink Master's room. Colours in pots were scattered around the floor in one corner.

'Fuck.' Zarifah cursed herself for forgetting that Ink Master would've finished the night's work hours ago and was now sleeping peacefully in the dorms. She didn't want to sleep.

She sat on the bench. Her room was the last place she wanted to be. She didn't want to face Nigil and have to please him. Not tonight, not ever again. Then if he turned up and she wasn't there, he would sell her for sure.

What should I do? Her mind was like a storm picking up options, examining them, then discarding them in fury. Closing her eyes, she tried to still the storm. Instead her mind drifted straight into blackness and accepted sleep instead of thinking.

***

Cold water thrown on her face jolted Zarifah awake. She came face-to-face with Nigil.

'Body's gone. But I don't know why you would be here when you're meant to be in your room.' Nigil's stare chilled Zarifah back to reality.

'I wanted my payment.'

Nigil threw a glass at the wall and Zarifah crouched as small pieces of glass flew around her body.

'No more for you. You'll never get your freedom.' He walked up to Zarifah and held her throat, lifting her slightly from the bench.

'Ink Master will be told not to tattoo you. You will be confined to your room. No scavenging. No practising. Torin is now in charge. You will do the main harvests each night. You can go to the Angel House each week.'

'You can't.' Zarifah managed to choke out the words before Nigil tightened his grip.

'I have. You have given me enough reason to kill you, legally. It would be all too boring to hand you to the Regulators. By the way, Kereta is gone. Sentinel, take her to her room.'

Nigil released Zarifah. She held her hands to her neck and struggled to inhale as the Sentinel pulled her from the bench and hauled her over his shoulder.

Zarifah tried not to cough, the movements hurt her throat and caused muscles in her back to contract against the small pieces of glass that must be embedded in her skin. Her tears flowed as she prayed to Her, desperate for help. No way could she get herself out of this mess. Having gotten so close to removing Nigil, she didn't know how he could've found out.

Her room had been searched. Zarifah stood in the middle of the mess, costumes lying on the floor, drawers partly opened and the simple mattress from her bed cut open and the insides pulled out. Forgetting the pain in her back and throat, she went straight to the secret compartments, praying to Her that Hayal hadn't told.

Panicked, she threw material, chains, hair products out of the way as she opened the last concealed compartment. There was the box from the Alchemist and the phials. Zarifah cried with relief. There was still some hope. She took out the hidden crystals from the previous night and placed them, with a blessing to Her, for extraction later.

The electronic sounds of someone punching in the code to her door brought her back and she put the objects away.

'Torin!' His face was swollen and he held his body upright and stiff as if he didn't want to move. He held the medical case and next to him Etana stood with a bowl of water. The door slid closed behind them.

'The price to pay was a little high this time,' said Torin.

Zarifah embraced him. But he didn't have the warmth towards her like before. She pulled away.

'He knows about Oren and the experiment. We mustn't give up. We've nothing to lose now.'

'How we can gain anything.' The condition of her own body was in a much better state than Torin's.

Zarifah pulled off her top to expose her bloodied back and

lay down on the lumpy mattress. Torin tweezered out the lodged pieces of glass as Etana rehung the costumes.

'Do you want some happiness?' asked Zarifah.

'No. Etana is here. Show some constraint,' said Torin. 'Is that all you can think about now? Consuming happiness?'

'We don't have to act on it. It would be better than a pill. Give us a pick me up.'

Torin threw the last of the bloodied sponge into the bowl. 'No.'

Zarifah pulled a shawl around her shoulders. 'Can you find out if Oren is alive?'

He sighed. Then nodded. 'I can't seem to resist you. I guess you'll still want this.' He handed her a small crystal, clear with smooth edges forming tabular sides.

'Small but a beauty,' said Zarifah.

'Be careful,' said Torin as he squeezed her hand, his eyes intense with care. 'Come on Etana, we have some practicing to do.' She kissed him.

Zarifah blew a kiss to Etana as she left with Torin.

Forcing herself up, she went to the compartment where the box was and began completing the extractions. As the phials filled with the harvested happiness, lightness and curiosity surrounded her. Her whole body pulsed with desire, with anticipation of the happiness that was being drained from each crystal into phials. It would help her to forget the mistake.

I should keep this for trading, or for Ink Master. Zarifah packed up the machine. *A gift for later.*

She imagined the smell spreading through her mind, her

body. The upwards spiral of ecstasy lifting her soul higher, leaving the pain behind. Before closing the compartment, she opened a phial and drank the contents.

Lying on her bed, she allowed her soul to be spirited away, the pure happiness like wings pushing her upwards. She relaxed into the intoxicating pulses of pleasure, her mind unravelling, new neurons firing with joy. The goddess filled Zarifah with waves of tingling excitement. She allowed herself to be lost in the rapture. It helped her to forget about what she planned to do tomorrow.

23

'Drink?' asked Zarifah. Nigil nodded. She poured him a shot; her fingers trembled a little as she tried to keep her nerves steady. Time had run out and Nigil was the only person she could think to use in the re-joining. *Then I won't have to kill him, but I'll still be The Collector.*

Nigil drank. The electronic clock ticked over. *Five minutes.* Her stomach fluttered. *Have I timed it right?*

Nigil slammed the glass back on the table causing Zarifah to jump. 'Another.'

Zarifah poured him another shot.

Oren walked into the office. 'Pure.'

'Really?' Nigil turned to him.

Zarifah took advantage and sprinkled the powder Oren had given her into the glass, and poured out another shot. 'Drink to that.' She handed him the glass again. Nigil slammed the drink back.

'You're lucky Senara came through,' said Nigil. He wiped his mouth.

'No luck.' Zarifah pursed her lips together. The incident with the dead patron had been covered up and this time there was no random inspection by the Regulators afterwards.

Nigil swayed. 'What did…?' He stood then stumbled back into his chair. 'You.' His eyes widened at Zarifah.

'Look how things have changed.' She stood waiting for the drugs to render him unconscious.

He went to get up but fell back into the chair. His eyes fluttered white and then he slumped, unconscious.

'Help me move him,' said Zarifah.

'If he dies they will just send another person like him. Nothing will change.' Despite his words Oren helped to move The Collector's body.

'I plan to take over,' said Zarifah puffing from the exertion of moving Nigil's body into the back room. Oren strapped him in and began attaching electrodes and patches to the side of his head and to his chest. *I will be different.*

'Is he secure?' asked Zarifah holding on to the bench to stop herself from collapsing.

'Yeah. Do you want me to start?'

'Yeah. Let's see if we can reunite his soul.'

'And if it works? What do we do with him?' Oren flicked switches and the machine hummed awake.

'Lock him downstairs.' Zarifah had her instructions from Her, but she wasn't about to kill. *Not after the patron the other night.* She'd gone too far then. *I won't this time.*

Electricity coaxed awake the soul crystal around Nigil's neck causing it to glow a bright pink.

'This is the tricky part. I have to set the electricity to shock so that the soul can be released. I still don't know how much to use,' said the Alchemist more for his own benefit.

Zarifah's fingers fidgeted around her own soul crystal. *Please work.* The Alchemist set the machine, took a deep breath and simply pressed the button.

Nigil's body arched forward. He screamed. Electricity exploded into his body. Oren swore as he frantically altered the settings and the familiar burnt smell began to diffuse out.

Oren tried again. This time Nigil's body didn't arch. A pink gas extended out from the crystal, just a small faint stream. Nigil gasped and the pink returned to the matrix.

'What's wrong?' The burnt smell intensified. *He's still breathing.*

'Nearly there.' His fingers worked the settings rapidly. 'One more try.'

This time the pink energy extended out from the crystal and into Nigil's chest. Like a pink snake it wound around the air. The pink rippled towards the body as if calling its mate to come out. Zarifah held her breath.

But nothing came up from the still body, just the empty rise and fall of the chest, becoming slower and slower.

'Can you do something?' whispered Zarifah.

The Alchemist shrugged. Once more he altered the settings.

An involuntary jump from Nigil's body caused the pink energy to shift upwards. Nothing was released from his body.

The energy floated back down like a translucent blanket enfolding the body as Oren tried again and again. Each time the room filled with the stench of burning flesh and the newly freed soul from the crystal faded in colour.

Nigil's body convulsed. Zarifah cringed as his arms and legs pulled against the straps. *Give in.* But he fought back at what they were doing to him. His body shook more violently. Skin around his wrists where the straps held him down began to bleed. Nigil continued to fight back, straining against the procedure. *Maybe it can't be put back together?* An acidic taste filled her mouth. *Her please let it work.* She forced herself to watch. The crystal holding his soul pulsed brilliant red and his head thrashed side to side. The smell of urine filled the room. Zarifah held her hand over her mouth and nose. Nigil's body jerked out of control, faster and faster.

With a final arch of his body and a raspy gasp, Nigil's body stilled. The last of his pink soul energy dispersed in the room. Darkness snaked out of his body and dispersed into the air.

'No wonder the newly escaped soul couldn't enter. He was too twisted and dark,' said Oren as he switched the machine off.

'Ah, I'm breathing in his soul,' said Zarifah holding her hand over her nose and mouth and swaying from the nauseating smell.

'The filters will clean the air soon enough,' said Oren.

Zarifah stood next to The Collector waiting, as if his eyes would open and he would slap her. She felt like a hunter standing over her prey that had been elusive for so long, but one that had finally succumbed to her play.

Shocked, she placed her hand around his throat searching for his life pulse. Finding nothing, she squeezed as if to act revenge on the master who had bruised her throat so many times before.

'You're not free yet,' said the Oren. 'The body is the easiest thing to remove here.'

Zarifah let go of the lifeless neck. She took his wolf pin from his shirt, a few pills and a laser gun. The Collector had finally been removed. The metal pin tingled cool in her hands. *I'm The Collector now.* Her skin prickled. She pinned it to her top near her heart.

Oren's hands stroked the bare skin between Zarifah's shoulders.

'There's work to do.' She moved away from him. 'Untie the body. We don't want others to know what we were really trying to do. The Regulators will be here soon enough,' instructed Zarifah once she was sure that she had removed anything of importance from Nigil.

'I want payment.'

Zarifah held up the small laser gun she had just removed from Nigil's body. 'I'll send you straight to Her, but I doubt that she'll let you in when you are now the one standing in the way of her return.' Power surged through her veins. Something changed inside of Zarifah when she'd taken the wolf pin. There was only one person she wanted to be intimate with and that was Torin.

'You need me to experiment,' said Oren, his words breaking nervously.

'You're replaceable.' She pulled her shoulders back. 'Are you going to help me or not?'

Oren lowered his eyes.

'Good, you talk to anyone about what happened here, and I will set you in the chair and see what experiments I can think up.' Zarifah hated the words she spoke. *I have to ensure I'm in control. It's the only way to bring Her back to Earth.*

'Put him down the chute.' *Food for the katners is more than he deserves.*

Zarifah walked into Nigil's office and booted up the console and slotted in his chip. Sitting in his chair, she felt the words of Her pushing through for attention.

She typed using trial and error to move through the system so that she could send a message to Senara. Her heart pumped as quickly as her fingers moved, adrenalin helping her.

She found the message bank and wrote the simple word, 'Done' along with the code. For a brief moment she wondered if that would be enough; there had been so much not said and could she really trust Senara; she was an Emotionless after all. Ignoring the screams of no from Her, she sent the message. There were too many people who she couldn't trust and she added Her to the list.

Pulling out her own chip, she reprogrammed the payment so that she would have enough flowers for her belt to be completed as well as storing the codes to the House. She now had access to the House money and was surprised to see how much Nigil had stockpiled.

The bastard. She realised that he didn't need the money

and that greed was his motivation in sharing her with Kade's House.

Her waist itched to have the last of the flowers added and instead of scrolling through images and notes of Nigil's about the management of the House, she removed the chips and shut down the system. Knowing that she was the only one who now had access gave her some peace, limited as it was.

A Sentinel opened the door and stepped in. 'I heard...' He stopped when he saw Zarifah.

'I'm the new Collector.' Her voice confident, she held her head high.

The Sentinel paused looking around the room. 'The Collector?'

'Yes.' Zarifah enjoyed this new power. 'I have the Regulators' backing.' She stood, fingering the laser gun on her hip. She liked the cold feel of the metal on her fingers. *Nothing is going to stop me now from helping to reincarnate Her.* 'You're to guard the room and let no one in.'

He nodded sharply.

This could be my only chance to have the last few flowers added. She went a few doors down to the Ink Master.

'Zarifah, my dear, your neck looks worse for wear,' said the Ink Master as he met Zarifah outside his work room.

'It's paid off.' Zarifah handed him her chip.

'You've been paid?' The Ink Master sounded suspicious.

'Yeah, well the neck?' Zarifah pointed to her reddened skin.

The Ink Master whistled long and soft. He looked at her sternly. 'Almost too good to be true?' he said motioning her to sit on the table. 'The first Soul Dancer to be free. What deal did you make with him?' He raised his eyebrow questioningly.

'I'm staying on for the House.' She suppressed a smile. *As The Collector.*

The needles began their electronic dance. 'Hope you haven't overstepped the mark.' His face close to her belly as he etched away freehand. The green vine joined around her waist decorated with blue forget-me-nots. His work was artistic and delicate.

Now that she was The Collector, Zarifah could hardly register that these last few flowers meant that she was free. It was really the wolf pin and Senara's support that freed her. *Come quickly Senara.* Zarifah didn't want to lose her position before the Regulator arrived.

'Done. You're free.' He turned off the tattoo machine. A chilly silence filled the room.

'You'll still see me.' Zarifah slipped off the table tentatively.

'Yeah right, you've no reason to keep coming to see an oldie like me.' The Ink Master cleaned the equipment.

Zarifah leaned over and kissed his forehead. 'You're wrong. There's plenty of reason.' Zarifah winked cheekily as she left the room, wishing she could tell the Ink Master more. She wanted to go and see Torin but she didn't want to answer his questions. *Will he be angry with what I've done?* She shook her head. *It's Her's work not mine, he can't be angry.*

24

'Enter,' said Zarifah. She swivelled on the chair and turned to face the door. She'd sat for hours waiting in the office.

Three Regulators walked in, bringing a void of emptiness as their grey-clothed bodies automatically sucked in the impure emotions lingering in the room. Senara stood with a man and woman behind her. Zarifah held onto the edge of the table to stop her hands from shaking.

'Leave us,' said Senara to the Sentinels. Zarifah swallowed hard.

'He's dead?' asked Senara, her face remaining expressionless.

Zarifah nodded.

'Well we have a new Collector here, congratulations.'

Zarifah smiled. A ripple of excitement sent the hairs on the back of her neck to standing.

'Here are the new codes for your House.' Senara handed over a chip. Zarifah's skin prickled with pleasure as their skin connected briefly.

'It's official then?' asked Zarifah, plugging in the chip to the computer and starting the transfer.

'Yes. But you belong to me now.' Senara walked over and pressed a laser to Zarifah's skull. Fear and rotting food smell spread from Zarifah's personal energy field.

'Ah, you are good at feeding me. Much better than Nigil.' Senara groaned in pleasure, sucking in the negative emotion. 'This is my House, for my feeding needs.' She pressed the end of the gun firmly to Zarifah's head. 'I'll make sure you keep the title of Collector.'

'I understand.' Zarifah didn't hesitate. This was what she'd been working towards with Her. *I'm free and I'm The Collector. I can handle Senara.*

'You can keep the other Regulators away?' asked Zarifah.

'That's the plan. The more emotional energy I have, the more bribes can be taken. Oh, and don't go making waves that I need to cover up. Nigil was good at making problems, I won't miss him.' She ran the gun down the side of Zarifah's cheek as if it were an extension of her fingers. Her other hand teased its way along the skin of Zarifah's chest.

'What's the quota?' Zarifah forced herself to talk. Her mouth dried.

'Ten emotions each night.'

'That's too much!'

Senara's fingers gripped the gun and pushed it into her head. 'You'll continue harvesting, and I expect the quota to be filled each night. I've such a hunger.'

Zarifah wanted to protest. The aim of all this was to restore

Her, and stop the blasphemy of the harvesting. Her emotions pulled away as Senara fed making it difficult for her to think.

'Now, let's go and announce the new leadership. I look forward to viewing the harvest tonight.' She leant close to Zarifah. 'And then we shall have our fun.'

Zarifah pursed her lips together and pressed the communicator. 'Dancers to the practice room.'

'Let's go then.' Senara put the gun away and motioned for Zarifah to follow.

What have I done? Zarifah's insides fluttered as she followed Senara. *This wasn't what I had in mind.* The little power she had tasted, she wanted back. But it seemed that Senara was the real boss of this House now and that scared Zarifah to the bone.

A strong current of nervous energy pulsed through the House as the dancers gathered. Zarifah stood near Senara.

'There's been a change of leadership,' announced Senara. Gasps of shock from the members of the House rippled the air. The emotional pull near The Regulators caused Zarifah to feel faint and she struggled against the current of energy they consumed.

'Zarifah is your new Collector,' informed Senara. The dancers bowed their heads as Zarifah stepped forward, her shawl wrapped tightly around her shoulders as if there was a new chill in the air. *I have to turn things around.*

'We will harvest well tonight to provide our guests with a feast they will remember,' said Zarifah ignoring the shocked expression on Torin's and Hayal's faces. 'These Regulators are who we truly serve and they will keep the others away.

'Torin is now the Soul Dancer,' announced Senara.

The challenge sparked interest from some of the dancers and Zarifah was annoyed that tonight may be her last dance. Her soul yearned to keep harvesting, even though she didn't want to dance like this. She really didn't want the other dancers to no longer complete the nightly harvesting and begin to learn the truth about the Soul Dancer faith. But Senara had taken control, and Zarifah was left struggling to think of a way to turn things around.

'Get ready for the performance,' demanded Senara.

The dancers hurried away. The whispers of shock and confusion annoyed Zarifah.

'Can you disguise yourselves tonight?' asked Zarifah. The three Regulators looked blankly back at her. 'The harvest is more fruitful without your presence. You may be a friend to this House, but most hate the Regulators.'

'There's a section for us near the bar where we can watch,' said Senara. 'Go and get ready for tonight.'

Zarifah bowed briefly and left the room. Dressing for the performance, Zarifah began a plan to hand out more crystals to the dancers, now she knew the high quota that had to be filled each night. She wrapped the black synthetic material around her breasts tying the ends halter neck style behind her neck and it cut into her skin. She secured the wolf pin in a fold of material then strung small metal balls around her belly. Tonight she wore tight black pants that were split above each knee ending in a ruffle above her ankle with a belt decorated with metal and plastic strips that hung down to mid-thigh.

Zarifah applied Kohl to her eyes, extending it out to a

point, shaping them more like almonds. The absence of the goddess was making her nervous. She added black and grey colour to the lids of her eyes, just enough to add a dark mystery. Reddening her lips, she felt ready to go out for the evening harvest as the Collector. *Given me strength to find a way through this, Her.*

Instead of going backstage with the dancers, she went to the bar area to make her first inspection as Collector. The lights had been dimmed to help patrons feel anonymous. Patrons of all species, mainly free emotional humans who were on the run from the Emotionless, sat at the bar or at the tables. Drinking in silence rather than to mingling with fellow travellers. Soft electronic music filled the background space of the room, helping patrons relax. Subliminal notes hidden in the music helped to keep them thirsty for the House liquor which helped them to remain clueless when their emotions were harvested. All dancers were immune to these notes to encourage the patrons to drink. It was part of the skill they held along with being able to steal emotions through dance.

'Keep their drinks full,' said Zarifah to the bar staff when she saw some patrons with empty jugs. They jumped at the sharpness of her voice.

'Come sit on my lap, sweetie,' said one.

'Don't talk to The Collector like that,' said the Sentinel. He punched the alien, who sprawled backwards, knocking surrounding chairs and hitting his head with a sickening crack on the floor. Blood oozed from his nose. Zarifah froze, surprised at the Sentinel's loyalty now to her. *I can get used to this.* She squared her shoulders.

The patrons stopped drinking, staring at her and the bleeding alien.

'Now I have your attention. I'm The Collector of the House. We are celebrating the change tonight, so drink up.' She signalled to the bar slaves to fill the drinks. 'Give out cigars. On the house for tonight.'

A few of the braver patrons cheered and held up their glasses to be filled. She moved around the space, checking for the Regulators. She couldn't find them. In the stink of the room, rotting emotions, cigarette smoke, and black desires, she had no hope of detecting the Emotionless with their scentless bodies. She couldn't find the void they usually created.

Zarifah could feel the patrons eyeing her as she moved between the tables. When the smells began to turn to putrid oranges she knew that some of the patrons were too attentive of her presence instead of losing themselves in the drink. Zarifah left, annoyed at herself for not predicting their response when they saw her dressed for the performance. She began to doubt that she had any control down here in the dungeons of the Earth. That she had only been a puppet for the hunger of Senara.

Side stage, Torin organised the dancers. He gave Zarifah a cool glance. Torin wasn't the only one who was distant towards Zarifah and her body prickled as if the temperature had dropped below zero.

So this is how it's to be. This is what it means to be the boss.

Wanting to exert her new title but overcome with the coldness, Zarifah put on a stern look. The expectation of being in charge and having the chance to be alone with Senara again were fading. She forced herself to stay and to begin her own inspection of the dancers.

Etana was dressed ready to dance. Zarifah was surprised that she was going to dance and that Torin would take such a risk. *I'd hoped to spare her from dancing.* She was about to question him when someone brushed her arm.

'Collector are you ready for the harvest to begin?' The Presenter asked Zarifah. His suit-like costume of dark green pin stripes looked out of place amongst the dancers.

'Yeah.' Zarifah's stomach and mind turned in opposite directions and Sentinel's hand helped to steady her. This was too much change. The feeling between the dancers was still cool as The Presenter began stirring the patrons with expectation.

'After the harvest and the extractions you are to meet here, everyone is expected. We will have our own celebration,' said Zarifah. *I need to stamp my authority on them.* But there was also something else. She wanted to give them a celebration, to sweeten them to her leadership.

'Sentinel, can you organise the bar and keep the liquor flowing after the harvest. Once the patrons have gone, get people to clean and pack away the tables and chairs and bring out the cushions and smoking pots,' said Zarifah quietly.

'Can't leave you.' He stood firm, his huge body towering over Zarifah.

'I just gave you an instruction.'

'Yeah and that Regulator, she threatened that if I left your side I'd be shot.'

'Fuck.' Her life was meant to be simpler when she became Collector.

'Right, you.' She pointed to a young male dancer who came off the stage, chest heaving as he tried to control his breathing. 'Go and bring me a bar staff-member.'

The boy ran off and Zarifah turned her attention to the dancing. Within seconds the familiar pull from the drumbeats and energy welled up inside her solar plexus. The desire to keep dancing was strong. She added her energy to the dance, guiding Etana to the patron with the strongest energy. The dancer didn't need much help. Etana danced as if she'd been performing for years. She controlled the energy around her like the more experienced dancers and walked from the stage without any internal conflict. Torin and Hayal moved to her side. A coldness spread over her body.

'Have you ever thought that maybe Her isn't meant to return?' Torin said as he positioned himself on the other side of Hayal.

'I don't know what is worse, that you killed Nigil, or that you have brought that shit into our House,' said Hayal. 'Doesn't it stink enough already down here?'

Zarifah ignored them as The Presenter waved the curtain up and the drums increased in volume. *They don't know what it's like.* She could sense the cinnamon. *Happiness.* It was like her whole body rumbled with hunger as her hips swayed in subtle figures of eight setting the metal she wore sounding like chimes. Torin and Hayal went out on stage to start the last harvest for the evening.

Zarifah checked the peephole to make sure that the patrons were filing out before making her way to the office. *My office. I will not be like Nigil.* She sat down on the chair and booted up the console. The room was stuffy and the basic furniture made the room feel large and unwelcoming. A place that was easy to leave, and one to dread entering.

'Send them in,' said Zarifah to the Sentinel, who let the first dancer enter. Dahra's costume was sparse, an opaque strip of black elastic material barely thick enough to cover her nipples and a low hanging skirt. She had danced well tonight; the crystals pulsed strongly around her neck. Her lean white body was toned from the dancing and she showed aptitude for controlling the energies.

Zarifah unclipped the collecting crystals using the new codes stored in the wolf pin. The warmth of the dark emotions trapped inside enveloped her as she handed them over to Oren for extraction.

Dahra stood, trying to contain her feelings but Zarifah sensed the coolness seeping from the dancer's heart. Zarifah thought the dancers of the House would've been happy at Nigil's end and embrace the chance to bring Her back.

'You want to say something?' asked Zarifah as she stood in front of the girl, wishing that the Alchemists would hurry up so that she could get this process over with and go and meet Senara. Zarifah wanted to take back the control Senara had taken, so she could run the House as she pleased.

'How could you?' Dahra whispered, taking up the invitation with hesitation.

'How could I what? Are you sure you really want to be questioning me when I'm about to give you your earnings for the night?'

'What about Her?' The frustration welled in her eyes. 'After all that you have taught us, you don't honour Her by making us dance.'

'Dahra, these things take time.' Zarifah clenched her jaw. 'Trust me, like you are now.'

'Pure, but it's fear.' Oren stomped back in the room and held the now empty crystals to Zarifah.

Zarifah clipped back the crystals, locking them in place either side of the moon shaped crystal that held part of Dahra's soul.

'One ladybird.' Zarifah traced the beginning of the series of insects with black and red backs around Dahra's waist. She knew that she was being overly generous but she was trying not to be like Nigil. And that was turning out to be more difficult than she had anticipated. 'You remember my generosity tonight. It won't be like this again. The dancing will stop soon.' Zarifah programmed Dahra's chip for one ladybird. She'd been hoping for her favourite emotion, but there was none of that from this girl.

'Go back to the stage and help prepare the room,' said Zarifah handing her the chip. Dahra nodded and left.

Senara strutted into the room. 'How's the extraction going? I am becoming hungry.'

'Just beginning. Do you want to stay?' Zarifah hoped

otherwise. *I want to go and find Torin, talk with him.* Heat flushed her cheeks. She really wanted to do more than that. *I have to talk to him so he knows I'm being forced to keep the nightly harvest.* 'I'm planning a celebration in the stage area to help the dancers with the transition. You can find all the entertainment and food you desire there perhaps?'

'There's only one who I want to feed with tonight,' said Senara quietly.

'This wasn't part of the deal.'

'What deal exactly? You are a slave, my slave, my dancer, to do with as I please. Now I have an entire House to keep me fed and with leftovers that will help me rise through the ranks of The Regulators.'

Zarifah stood, the words stabbing her body as she realised that there was another game to play, no longer with Nigil, now with Senara. *It will just be a little while. When Her is reincarnated, then things will change.*

'Let's process the harvest, we can talk later.'

Zarifah hurried the remaining dancers through with the Regulators watching, the red pills reducing her headache and she used the new energy to process the harvest.

'Good start,' said Senara as she tallied the takings on her own handheld electric console. 'I want more in the future.'

Zarifah swallowed her protest. 'You'll keep sending patrons with something worth harvesting?'

'If you keep the quota filled, I'll send you some extras. Now let's go to this celebration, I am so hungry.' They went down to the practice room.

Loud music played, the drummers making their own unique rhythm with a freedom they had never been given before. The young dancers were back in the dorms. Many had wasted no time with the chance to drink and forget. The stage area was full of cushions that spilled out to where the patrons had been sitting only hours ago. Half naked bodies lazed around drinking, eating, smoking, and touching. Given new freedom, the House members made the most of the night. The cook had put out some food to nibble. Smoke rings formed in the far corner. Ecstasy rippled through the room without any happiness, a primal energy of lust, and only Zarifah longed for the spiciness to be added.

Some of the dancers stiffened as the Regulators approached. Others were engrossed in flesh, and didn't care as they lost themselves in the pleasures. The younglings were in bed away from the celebrations for the adult dancers.

Zarifah directed the Regulators to one side, hoping that they wouldn't disrupt the pleasures of the House members. She wanted them all to enjoy themselves tonight, as much as one could when you lived with only part of your soul free and you were forced to abuse the sacred skills of life by stealing emotions from others.

Torin approached them and bowed his head as he held out a flask of Spirit to Senara.

'You do well to please,' she said taking the flask. Senara took a small sip and then handed the flask to the man behind her. 'Not my preferred drink.'

Torin bowed and turned to leave.

'Wait.' Senara's hand touched his shoulder and jealousy

rose in heat through Zarifah's entire body. She didn't know who to be more jealous of, Torin for playing a great move, or Senara for giving him attention.

'Soul Dancer.' She looked at her before realising Senara wasn't talking to her. The heat turned to anger. Senara had made her decision and the game changed once more.

'Are the rooms upstairs ready?' asked Senara.

Zarifah nodded.

'Go and make your choice.' Senara signalled to the Regulators who moved out into the mass of increasingly naked bodies.

'I've made mine.' Senara stroked Torin's muscular chest. Zarifah suppressed the words of protest that were forming. She wanted to push Senara away to stop her from touching Torin. *We're meant to be together now.* But so far it seemed just as difficult as ever for Torin and her to find time together.

'You have responsibility here,' said Senara as she linked her arm with Torin's and walked towards the stairs. 'We'll meet in the morning.'

The false void moved away as the Regulators left. People continued drinking and absorbing each other as if nothing had happened. Someone handed her a flask of liquor and Zarifah drank as she watched the frivolity, angry that she had missed out on her own pleasure.

She was tempted to take out the phial and drink the intoxicating emotion now and then join with the others on the cushions. The phial, small and unassuming, was warm against her body. Odourless, she knew what it would smell like once consumed.

Zarifah sipped at the liquor drink. Her mind blurred as the feeling of rapture built within her. She saw Oren dancing. There was still no happiness around him or any of the other dancers. What they were releasing tonight was more primal, the root of humanity.

'Collector,' yelled Hayal. A title she now despised.

'Come and dance.' Hayal was intoxicated and her chest sweaty from the drink and exertion of exploring the flesh of others.

'No,' said Zarifah even though she longed to after the night had taken so many unexpected turns.

'Look how events have favoured you.'

Yeah look. Zarifah sipped her drink. *Torin is with Senara.*

'Come on.' Hayal dragged Zarifah to the centre of the dancing. Zarifah cursed the Sentinel for not stopping the girl but he was already lost to the atmosphere.

The heat alone was intoxicating. Naked bodies were pumping together in time with the music, in and out, the movements natural and erotic. Without wanting to, she soon found herself grinding with Hayal and another dancer. Their skin sweaty and the salt an addictive temptation on her tongue.

'Knew you needed to loosen up,' said Hayal, her breath hot and sweet from the liquor drink. Zarifah kissed her, holding back from losing herself before she turned away smiling and found other lips to kiss as she moved through the dancers, tasting their bodies as they tasted hers. Pleasuring each other as the drum pounded out the rhythm they wanted people to move to. For once she was one of them, a slave with no title.

Keeping herself anchored and not surrendering to the drink or the beat, Zarifah kept moving between people. Aware of what she was doing, she refused to lose control but gave herself permission to be free and surrender to the pleasures of the night. There was no spiciness in the air, nothing so exotic produced between those she touched and kissed. Only the connection of humanness was awakened and the primal basic urge that all yearned for. For hours her mind, body and soul were joined with others who knew her heartache, and their fingers and tongues and bodies massaged the hurt away. As she in return dissolved their pain.

The energy gripped Zarifah's soul, begging for her to surrender and take part in the atmosphere with the other members of the House. She resisted until, like a string carrying too much weight, she broke and joined herself whole with the others in this tasting of sweat and flesh. Sixty bodies moved as the energy pulsed through them like waves, rippling them with pleasure individually and causing them to move as one.

The earthy energy in the room wrapped them together in one blanket supporting them as they surrendered. This was how they were meant to use their skill, to ease the pain of others, to help them to find the source of their discomfort. Here, as slaves, they knew the source, a continuous cycle of pain that had made them forget what it was like to be happy. For once they used their skills on each other in an orgy of healing and the Earth answered their call and pulsed with them, releasing some of its own pain and pollution for the transformation.

There was a slow peak in atmosphere tonight, a long ascension, a lasting orgasm. Everyone wanted to mount such unusual energy and they worked with their skill to maintain their desire. Everyone opened to each other to help them receive help until all had their pain taken away and they could relax in each other's arms and rest. Everyone was equal as all humans were. Forgetting that tomorrow they would have to face their world again, to remember that they were slaves, that their souls were split and the opportunity to restore Her was fading. They kept moving and tasting and massaging with their bodies until they were exhausted. Sweaty bodies lay on cushions, breathing a calmness many hadn't experienced for years.

Eyes closed, they slept deeply. Bodies intertwined and united in what it meant to be human—they cared—something no emotion could produce yet was needed as the catalyst.

Zarifah stroked the person's stomach next to her as she moulded her body to theirs and someone else did the same to her. Her body responded and she those around her rippled with the same response as the pleasure moved like a snake around the resting bodies.

She rested her head on a cushion. Her mind calm and unable to play the games it was so used of doing. *I must remember this.* She enjoyed the newly found peace.

25

Torin found Her, by the side of a barren lake. A thunderstorm hung heavy behind them. An etheric wind made it hard for him to hold his form here in the astral plane. Zarifah's actions forced him to seek guidance. He could no longer trust her and this broke his heart. There was only one thing left to do—ask Her for guidance.

Her, dressed in a transparent black robe, materialised. Wings moved with the flow of the rising wind.

'Mother.' He knelt down at her feet.

'My ever-faithful son.' She bent down and helped him to stand. 'What brings you here?'

'My love for you.' He paused and looked into her eyes, unsure if to continue.

'Something else? A troubled heart perhaps?' Her's voice soothed Torin's fear. 'My son, I've heard it all before, nothing can shock me.'

'I fear... I think... Zarifah's lost her path.'

Her placed her hand on his shoulder and smiled. The storm

rumbled closer. The black hole, the Abyss, wanted her energy, wanted to suck her soul. Her had cheated the darkness for too long.

'Zarifah's no longer doing your work. She seeks her own power and glory.' Torin lowered his eyes, his heart heavy with betrayal. He loved Zarifah, but what she did was wrong.

'My child, you've done well to seek me out.' She brushed her fingers over his cheek, down his neck and over his toned chest. 'You'll be well rewarded.' She smiled sweetly. 'To reincarnate I need a body. A female's. It sounds like you've found the perfect volunteer.'

'I don't think Zarifah will be willing.'

'She won't have a choice.' Her stood to full height and Torin bowed. 'I'll make sure of that.'

***

Zarifah walked past the revelries from the night before. Dancers were stirring and some beginning to clean up. Would repeating such a night in the future hold as much power. The night, whatever had happened, had made everyone closer and more united. *Peace.* Zarifah hadn't felt so calm for years.

The cold room held nothing of the tranquillity outside. She booted up the computer. Guilt stabbed at her solar plexus. *I didn't want to make them dance.* She drummed her fingers on the desk thinking. Things hadn't turned out like she had planned.

'The experiment to reverse the split is ready.' Oren interrupted her thoughts.

'I don't have anyone to test the machine on.' She paused to think. *No I do.* 'Let's get started.'

Oren had the chair ready and the electronics responded to his touch with beeps of pleasure. Zarifah took a deep breath. *Will this work?* The risk was death.

Zarifah sat in the chair.

'You can't be serious!' said Oren.

'Get me ready.' She settled back into the chair.

'This is suicide.' He ran his hands through his blond thinning hair.

'It's my chance to change the future.'

'You've been warned.' Oren moved around, attaching electrodes to Zarifah's head and chest.

'You have to remove the metal,' said Oren, pointing to the laser gun at her waist. She reluctantly handed it over and then began to unpin the wolf.

'Wait,' said Zarifah as Oren was about to take the metal pin. 'There's an important step to do first.' Zarifah finally used the pin to unlock the electric codes in the tear shape crystal.

'Maybe that's why it didn't work before,' said Zarifah.

'Maybe.'

'I expect those things to be untouched through this process,' warned Zarifah as she rested back. 'We could also do with a more comfortable chair. One with padding.'

'Ready?' He looked up, his forehead wrinkled, his eyes reflected doubt.

'Get on with it,' said Zarifah. She closed her eyes. *This will work. It has to.*

Oren pushed the screen and a pulse of electricity shot through the electrodes causing Zarifah's body to arch momentarily before collapsing back onto the chair.

Pink soul energy eased from Zarifah's chest and weaved around towards the matrix, changing colour as the soul energy inside, a soft yellow colour, was coaxed out of its prison. Tentatively the yellow energy left its cage, extending its own tendrils to form a double helix shape of two colours above Zarifah's throat.

Winding and winding, the pink and yellow weaved the shape back on itself leaving no gaps of air. Tighter and tighter the colours joined as if they were creating their own primal dance, as if they were finding each other for the first time. The colours blended into white and in slow graceful swirls returned to the body they had been dancing above, entering through her open mouth. For a moment Zarifah's body glowed white.

'Beautiful,' whispered Oren as the last of the energy dissipated into Zarifah's chest. She gasped as if she'd been holding her breath the whole time. Sitting up, she coughed, her hand clasping her throat. The tear shaped crystal now black and dead. Intensity punched into her stomach. She leaned forward and dry-retched. She pulled at the electrodes.

'Hold on there,' Oren said softly, trying to get her to slow down. 'Has it worked?'

'Yes.' Zarifah slumped overwhelmed by the intensity of emotions coursing through her. *I feel alive.* She held onto the arms of the chair to steady herself. *We can start re-joining souls now. Her's work can finally begin.*

Zarifah slipped from the chair, grabbed the gun and pin, then walked uneasily back to the office. Her vision blurred and refocussed a number of times before she collapsed into the chair. *Finally progress. It will help the dancers forgive me.*

'You can't just go in.' Zarifah heard the Sentinel yelling outside the office.

'She will see me now.' The door opened and Torin walked in. Anger rippled around him and stirred Zarifah's desire for him.

'So how was Senara?' She raised an eyebrow.

'You know, so why ask?' He paused. 'Your anger is strong, in smell and energy, so much so we could put you out and harvest you tonight. What have you done?' He hesitantly stepped towards the desk and tilted his head questioningly.

Zarifah anger subsided knowing that Torin hadn't a choice to be with Senara. She could see her words had hurt him and he was pained by what he'd done. *Like me.*

Cinnamon tones began to pulse from Zarifah. She gasped at the intensity of such energy now that her soul was one. It flowed from her body and the familiar rise of pleasure tempted her on an ascent towards ecstasy.

The passion of anger in Torin's eyes changed; they softened with the cinnamon smell that intoxicated them both. He kissed her, the taste of the happiness urged him to play with her lips and tongue with a newly found desire as he lowered himself onto her lap.

Zarifah moved with his rhythm as if this was their first

time, as if the united soul that flowed in her presented something new to explore, an easier path to thrill each other in both body and soul.

Torin's fingers had developed a new tenderness from the experience of last night and he used them to send Zarifah's skin prickling with delight causing an increase in the intensity of the odour of cinnamon.

Spurring each other on, their bodies pumped together making a bridge for their souls to cross. Leaving their bodies so they could twist with each other, mixing and tasting the etheric joy, allowing them to find their way upwards towards rapture. There they snaked around each other, holding them together tightly. Invisible molecules of pleasure shot rapidly between their bodies and souls reinforcing the tension, building it tighter and higher.

Zarifah's energy expanded in the newly found freedom. But there were the scars of the past that weighed her soul, hardened parts like calluses on the skin, always limiting how far she could go. At the peak they held each other in rapture for what felt like minutes looking into each other's soul and seeing themselves, knowing that they were held in joy, love and goodness.

With a gasp of surprise, the bliss created collapsed, sending them tumbling back breathless to their own bodies. The bridge between them crumbled as they returned to being two with only the memory that for a brief moment they had managed to create a chemical reaction binding them as one.

Tasting the fading spiciness on each other's lips, they

completed the separation, trying to keep hold of the joy as it faded away.

'Your soul crystal is black. Are you going to tell me what you did?' said Torin. He caressed her body tenderly.

'I re-joined my soul. Surely you can guess that.' Zarifah ran her hands over his chest. Her body stirred willingly to go again with him.

'How are you going to keep this a secret?'

Zarifah pulled away, realising that the black crystal around her neck was going to be difficult to conceal from The Regulators. She may be free but soon she would be dead. 'I can get a similar looking crystal easy enough.' *She hoped.*

'So what are you going to do?' Torin pulled her back into his arms.

'Look for volunteers to re-join their souls,' said Zarifah, resting into his chest.

'What about the harvest?'

'We continue harvesting,' said Zarifah. 'We have to.' She felt him go cold. *He doesn't approve.*

'Her is waiting for her dancers to be free of the burden of harvesting.'

'Senara is forcing us.' Zarifah's voice was firm and business like.

'And you are letting you.'

'Only until I can think of a way to remove her without bringing all the Regulators here demanding our lives.' Zarifah playfully pushed at Torin to get him to move from the bed. 'We have a harvest to prepare for tonight.'

'The title of Collector means you can cancel the

performance tonight.' Torin grabbed Zarifah playfully by the waist. She kissed him. The taste of cinnamon only a memory as their lips met. *I can't.* She couldn't say no to Senara. Besides the House needed the emotions from the harvest for trade. 'Not tonight. The dancers only have to continue for a little while longer.'

A shadow passed over Torin's face. 'I don't like this, Zarifah.'

'Me neither.' But she couldn't stop. *Not now. Not until I have this House secure.* Besides, the power tasted good. She wasn't going to give it up.

'You'd better reconsider seriously,' said Torin.

Zarifah didn't take his warning to heart. Instead she kissed him, enjoying her whole soul beginning to meld with his once more.

26

'Time is running out. We have to keep pushing to reverse the process,' said Zarifah. 'Which is why I sent for O'yal. We have to keep trying.'

A Sentinel entered with O'yal in his arms.

'Give him to Torin,' said Zarifah. The Sentinel handed O'yal to Torin and they went to the alchemy rooms.

'I don't know that's going to be a good idea,' said Oren as Torin placed the boy on to the chair. 'His soul was split not that long ago. It will be too much for the youngling.'

'We have to try,' said Zarifah firmly as she helped to strap the unconscious boy into the chair. His star shaped crystal still pulsed a light red. Oren moved in and stuck the electrodes to the boy's chest and head before returning to plug away at the screen to charge the machine.

'Who takes responsibility for his death?' asked Oren.

'Just make sure you do your part correctly,' said Zarifah leaning on the metal bench. 'This worked for me, it should work for him, especially since it has only been a few hours since his soul was split. The connection should still be there, each half yearning for the other should make the re-joining a success.' She stepped forward and unlocked the soul crystal around O'yal's neck. *This time it will work.*

'Stand back.' Oren waited for them to move away before releasing the burst of electricity. The boy's body arched upwards, causing the belts on his wrist and ankles to dig into his flesh, opening the marks that were initially made when his soul was split. A black cloud seeped out above him as his body collapsed on the chair. The darkness swirled around, searching for the other part of the soul.

'It's the wrong colour,' said Oren. 'Yours was pink. It's not going to work.'

'Told you,' said Torin. 'You are so reckless with the risks.'

'The soul in the crystal hasn't come out. Give another burst.' Zarifah tried to remain hopeful as she stopped herself from praying to Her. She wasn't about to beg to a goddess who had left her.

'If I do, it may be too much.'

'Do it.'

Oren took a deep breath and fired the machine again. This time there was a release of a small amount of pink energy from the crystal before the blackness consumed it and the room began to smell of burning flesh.

'Ah, not again,' said Yanni as he entered the room covering his mouth. 'It took ages to clean the last mess.'

'Quiet,' said Oren as he punched the machine to shut down. The putrid smell caused them all to gag.

'How are you going to explain this one?' said Torin as he coughed into his hand, trying not to breathe.

'I'll handle it. Wrap him up and take him to the storage area. As far as you all know he didn't survive the split. And make sure you get rid of that burnt smell so there are no questions.' Zarifah kept her hand over her mouth while Oren and Yanni wrapped up the body and sprayed him down to remove the smell.

'What a waste,' said Torin.

'He was wasted as soon as he was split.'

'I don't sink as low as you.'

'I told you I'd do what it takes to restore Her. This is what it looks like.'

Torin shook his head as the boy was zipped into a green bag.

***

'Enter,' said Zarifah at the knock on the door. The Ink Master walked through with his black medical bag. She smiled at the old man who had inked her skin over the years. She almost missed the sessions now that her belt was completed.

'There's rumours,' said the Ink Master as he began to load the syringe. Zarifah sat on a stool, her arm exposed waiting for the familiar jab to protect against conception and diseases. The House had been clean and she intended to keep it that way.

'About what?'

'About you. How you're not any better than Nigil. How you lied about trying to restore Her.' He jabbed the needled into her muscle and began injecting the clear liquid.

'Yeah, well people will complain.' Zarifah held her finger over the spot to stop the bleeding while Ink Master began to load two more syringes. *I have to work out why things went wrong with O'yal. What was different.* 'I gave them a celebration.'

'The other night fades from their memories…'

The celebration. That was the difference. I wonder… Her mind pieced together the different soul re-joinings. *It worked for me because I felt at peace. I was happy. Sort of. Plus I had unlocked the soul crystal.*

'…They believed in you, that you would implement change. They don't now.' He closed the medical bag and stood to leave. 'I thought I should tell you, before it's too late.'

'Thank you.' Zarifah pulled down her sleeve. *I know what to do now.* And it had nothing to do with stopping the dancers from harvesting. She needed to have a lot of happiness to harvest first. *Then they can stop.*

***

'Here, I've something for you.' Zarifah took out a phial of happiness. She longed to drink it all herself but she wanted to prove that the process could be reversed, then the others would follow her.

'It tastes like nothing but will warm your heart.' Zarifah

held the phial to the Etana's lips, who hesitated before opening her mouth and drinking the liquid. Her body immediately converted the liquid into the energy of happiness and the spiciness made Zarifah's head spin. She held Etana close, savouring the smell.

'There's a special gift I have for you,' said Zarifah. 'Come on, it'll be fun.'

Zarifah took Etana by the hand and led her to the Alchemist's room.

Even though Etana was in a state of bliss, the Sentinel had to force her onto the chair and hold her down while Oren strapped her in. Zarifah tried to whisper words to soothe the girl, but she was drained by the desire to consume more of the happiness and she just wanted the experiment completed. To know if it would work. Out of sheer stubbornness she refused to pray to Her and ask for a blessing for what was about to be done.

'Etana, this will work if you are relaxed and happy. Allow yourself to rise with the energy that you consume and forget about the memories of this room. I am going to make you whole again.'

Zarifah stroked the girl's hair as she signalled to Oren to begin getting the machine ready. Etana closed her eyes.

'Stand back,' said Oren and Zarifah stood back and found herself holding her breath. Forcing away any doubt that this wasn't going to work and how could she do this to someone so young.

Etana's body arched with a pulse of electricity and the familiar pink energy rose from her body and her soul crystal at the same time. Zarifah clasped her hands together. *Please Her.* In a cloud above her body, the two shades of pink swirled together until they were uniform in colour. The shape of a snake formed, twisting gracefully in the air, performing its own beautiful dance, before it spiralled back down into the heart space of Etana.

'It worked!' said Zarifah relieved that the girl breathed and was now whole.

'Now we know, too dark a soul can't be re-joined,' said Oren, shutting down the machine.

'Then yours will be forever split,' said Zarifah as she began to untie Etana. The scent of happiness had faded and the girl looked exhausted.

'This is our secret, Etana. This is what I hope for all the dancers here.'

'But Her said it was too late,' said Etana, her words slurred as if it was an effort to focus.

'Her spoke to you?'

'She said you should stop, you've lost your way. This isn't what she wanted.'

'She wants us to remain split? You talk nonsense.'

'She said it's too late, for Her and for you.' Etana slumped back into the chair unconscious, leaving Zarifah staring at the child in disbelief.

'Commiserations on your success, Collector,' said Oren.

'Shut it and give her a new crystal.' Her soul crystal was as black as Zarifah's had been and she took it off and kept it for herself. A fake one now hung around her neck.

'Give her some sedatives and take her to my room. Have

one of the Sentinels keep watch.' She returned to her office and sat planning the evening. There was no way she was going to stop now. The goddess had been clear. *Her wouldn't change the plan.* It didn't make sense. She turned the pills Oren had given her around in her fingers. *This might work.* There was a chance she could deal with Senara. And give the dancers another great party. *Then re-join their souls.*

***

'Is Senara here?' asked Zarifah as she left the room bumping into the Sentinel.

'Yeah, she's watching the harvest with two others.'

'The usual two?'

The Sentinel nodded. He walked behind Zarifah as she stormed towards the stage area.

Torin calmly organised the dancers. 'Torin I've got something to tell you.'

'Not now, Zarifah.' His blue eyes cool as he looked at her. 'I've got to concentrate, and we have one less dancer which boils my blood.'

Zarifah lowered her eyes and the putrid smell of guilt wafted around her. That was her own fault, but she had made amends for it. The youngling walked on the stage pretending to be confident.

'It's Etana.' Zarifah paused as Torin rearranged the costume on Dahra to expose more flesh. 'I've re-joined her soul.'

'Yeah right.' The sarcasm in his voice hurt. 'You were a freak chance.'

'It worked.'

'Where is she? Is she crazed from the process? It's too risky.' Torin struggled to keep his voice down.

'Sleeping in my room. I know why it didn't work with O'yal. The soul has to be lightened beforehand, which mine was from the celebration. If there's too much darkness, the process won't work.'

'So how did you manage that with Etana?' Torin looked around to make sure the other dancers were getting ready.

'Happiness.' Zarifah smiled and lifted her chin up a little.

'And what now? You plan to have everyone here in this hell hole happy and then willing to try if the process can be reversed? Ignoring the very real fact that the process may kill them?'

'Yes.'

'This isn't what Her wanted,' said Torin, his body blazed with anger.

'But it will free us.'

'Will it?'

His words sent a shiver down her spine.

'Tonight is the perfect time. We can have another celebration, the Regulators can feast. They will lose themselves long enough for us to take them. Then we can ask who will follow Her and the process can be reversed.' Zarifah could barely breathe at the prospect of her plan finally coming together.

'You think that the people here will just walk into the room where their soul was divided and The Regulators will allow us? You've really lost your mind, more evidence not to reverse the process.'

'Will you support me?'

'Zarifah, this is too much.'

'Please?' She held his arm, and a faint cinnamon smell danced between them.

'I won't stand in your way.' He sighed and leant down and kissed her forehead, then returned to organising the dancers.

Zarifah walked to the bar area, slipping between the stinking patrons. The cauldron of emotions was thick with the usual anger and fear. There wasn't going to be much of a harvest, but Zarifah didn't care, things were going to be different after tonight.

She took a jug of water, knowing the Regulators would refuse to drink the liquor. Breaking the pills, she sprinkled the white powder into the liquid. Swirling the water to help the ingredient dissolve, she grabbed three cups. The chemicals in the water should be concentrated enough to do more than make someone sleep.

Tonight Zarifah felt the void and knew where the Regulators watched. The Presenter stood on stage preparing the audience for the last dance. The drums sounded like heartbeats in the background, the life pulsing in the room.

'Finally,' said Senara. Zarifah entered the concealed room where the Regulators were watching.

'Let me serve you,' said Zarifah bowing her head and gracefully pouring out the water. She made sure her fingers brushed the cold skin of Senara as she handed her the cup.

'Yeah you are a problem, lucky I like you.' Senara ran her

hand along Zarifah's arm sending shivers of pleasure with the light touch. 'I will more than enjoy your service tonight after all this trouble of another body to hide.'

Zarifah poured the remaining water into the cups. The Regulators drank in one big gulp and consumed her plan. Sitting next to Senara, she couldn't see the two Regulators behind her but she heard their breathing slow as the dancing began. *It will soon be different.*

Torin's skin glistened from the exertion of the controlled movements, his body tinged with purple bruising around his back and chest. The alcohol-affected patrons tried to focus in awe, wishing they could have him, thinking the dancer had something they wanted.

Senara, mesmerised by the movements Torin made, leant forward, trying to keep herself awake. Unaffected by the dance, Zarifah sat waiting, her eyes watching Senara, the person who stood in her way of success. The familiar vacuum around her weakened as the Regulators began to fall asleep. But Senara was stronger, and her eyes remained opened.

The three dancers enticed the audience to admire their bodies, rolling their bellies in time with the drums. Their arms floating in the air tasting the emotions as they secretly searched for the energy that would provide the highest payment. The drumming became faster and louder. Hayal's figure haunted the stage in the smoky light, her white skin illuminated in the lighting.

Torin danced from the stage towards the winged alien. He began the harvest dance.

'He's good,' said Senara. 'Better than you.' Her body swayed. 'You've given me something?'

'You asked too much.' Zarifah stood ready, hand on the sickle around her waist. Senara tumbled from the chair. Zarifah took the sickle from her belt and slashed at the throat of the Regulator. Her movement was quick and the copious blood flowing from the cut showed the main artery had been cut.

Senara tried to hit back, but she lost her balance. Zarifah swiftly moved out of the way. The Regulator held her throat in an attempt to stop the bleeding.

The blood made it slippery for Zarifah to keep her grip and hold Senara's arms, but she remained on top, determined to keep her position. Senara managed to bring her leg around and kick Zarifah in the back, causing her to loosen her grip. But she had lost too much blood and the drugs made her movements weak.

The drumbeat quickened, signalling the peak of the harvest. She held onto Senara, one who represented all the Regulators who had forced her into this business, who had ripped apart her soul, and made her use the sacred teachings to steal emotions for their own food. The smell of anger mixed with the earthy smell of blood in the room and Zarifah allowed her energy to take the life of woman.

The drumming stopped. The resonance of the sound rippled around the room, fading with the completion of the harvest as Senara's body convulsed in a last attempt to live. Muscles twitched, echoes of her own life seeping out silently as her soul broke free, without colour, without emotion. It left as if it had never been there.

Zarifah pulled back Senara's neck, causing the blood to flow more. She didn't want to make a mistake. The noises outside the room indicated that the patrons were leaving. With bloodied hands and chest she stood, her bare feet in the pooled blood, her sickle lost somewhere in the room. *Freedom. Sweet freedom.*

'I trusted you,' said Zarifah. 'I found a way to free myself. And the others.'

'Sentinel,' said Zarifah.

'Collector, are you Okay?' asked the Sentinel. His eyes widened and his jaw dropped when he saw Zarifah with blood-stained hands.

'Yes.' Revenge had been taken using her own hands and the blood of another made her hungry to finish the plan.

'Get someone to tie up those two, and bag her.'

He didn't move. 'Now.' The Sentinel nodded before rushing off. Zarifah wiped the blood from her hands on Senara's jacket, before her stained fingers began searching pockets. She took the chips, pills, and portable communicator and lasers, everything and anything that could be of use. The Sentinel entered with two other male dancers. They trembled at the sight of the blood-covered Collector searching the bodies.

'Make sure they are kept drugged,' instructed Zarifah as she stood, barely able to hold her loot. She left bloodied footprints walking to the stage area to find someone else to send for the dancers.

'What have you done?' said Hayal. She looked white with shock.

'Gained my freedom and everyone else's here,' said Zarifah placing the larger items on the edge of the stage.

'The Regulators will be here in hours,' said Hayal, her fear becoming her scent.

'No, because they don't know Senara was here, nor will they.' Zarifah counted on Senara not telling anyone that she was using this House for her own means. *It buys us time.*

'We need to surrender,' said Hayal.

'No,' said Zarifah. 'Go and get Torin and summon everyone. We're having a party.'

Holding her cheek, Hayal rushed off to do as she'd been told. Zarifah instructed the people to start preparing the room for the party. *Soon they would be free.* There were some hesitant yells of excitement as tables and chairs were removed. No one said anything as the three bodies were carried away.

'Zarifah are you Okay?' asked Torin as he came from the back of the stage. He jumped down and hugged her, the crystals around his neck pulsing with spiciness, stirring the desire in Zarifah to taste their energy. Resting her head on his shoulder, she allowed herself to relax and breathe in the remnants of his harvest.

'Stay here,' said Zarifah as she forced herself to pull away. A layer of blood now tainted his toned chest. She entwined her fingers with his as if that would ensure he wouldn't leave. She knew what she wanted but the spiciness fogged her mind, invisible tentacles entering and weaving like worms around her brain searching for the happiness that would help them dance in the clouds.

Slaves of the House settled on the stage, with cushions and flasks of Spirit. They looked scared, the fear causing the room to smell worse than when the patrons were here. In the nervous energy they sat waiting.

'You're free,' said Zarifah. 'The Regulators won't be bothering us for a while. We'll have to pretend to still be under their control. But by the time they come we will be a strong force.'

Looks of doubt mixed with their fear kept them all silent.

'I'm Collector of this House. We can begin to infiltrate other Houses. We can return Her, now.' Zarifah allowed her voice to become more animated to try and get a response from people.

'How do we know?' yelled someone.

'Yeah, you sold us out when you became Collector.'

'Why should we trust you now?'

'I've taken care of the Regulators that were here, Senara's blood is on my skin alone. Now we can celebrate, and then you have the chance to have your souls united.'

People began talking.

'You trying to kill us?'

'The Collector's crazy.'

'I've tried it on myself,' said Zarifah. 'My soul is united and I give you the chance to do the same.'

'You lie, Collector.'

'There's more of us than you.'

'It will work,' said a young voice from the back of the stage. Etana walked forward. 'I'm whole once more.'

Etana pushed between them as if she was a goddess herself, enchanting them with her innocence, helping them to remember, to believe that they could be whole, they could be happy. 'This is your chance to bring Her back. Why don't you take it?' Etana spoke softly as she walked between them on the stage. Gradually words of agreement were whispered as Etana walked up to Zarifah. She took out the blackened crystal and handed it to Etana. 'You have something of mine.'

Zarifah took out the blackened crystal, which hung on a thin metal chain.

'Don't forget,' said Zarifah as she handed it to Etana. With shaking hands, Etana clipped the crystal around her neck.

'Let's celebrate,' said Zarifah holding up Etana's hand, the blackened crystal shining in the dimming light as the music began playing and jugs were filled with Spirit.

The music and the liquor loosened the last of the doubt as the dancers began to move like they had once before. This time they were determined to remember.

'Let's dance,' said Hayal as she took Etana back to the group.

Zarifah smiled as everyone joined in. Her plan was finally coming together. In a few days, they would only be dancing for themselves and no longer having to complete the harvest.

'Join me?' Torin's words broke her thoughts of the plans she was making for the future of the House, her House. 'Some enhancement?' He held up a phial. The spicy smell caught in her throat and her mind spun. He held the phial to her lips and drank. The spiciness filled her body, blurring her senses and sending her on a cloud of bliss. Then suddenly it was as if she crashed back down to earth. Something hard and sharp ripped at her stomach. Zarifah doubled over, clutching at her waist. 'What have you done to me?' She looked up through blurred vision at Torin.

'Her's work.' He stepped back and crossed his arms. 'The final part of the plan.'

Zarifah gasped for breath as agony cut at her insides. She fell onto her knees.

There was always one more step to climb. The voice of Her didn't shock Zarifah as she breathed in the presence of the goddess, welcoming Her, the boost of energy claiming her mind in a trance.

I needed a body to return. Her's voice tore through her mind once more. The image of the goddess floated beside Zarifah, laughing. Zarifah tried to speak but there was pressure on her neck and she saw Her's hands holding tight. *You're not strong enough to return me to Earth, I had to find someone else. But your body will do nicely.*

Zarifah's mind grabbed at Her, holding tight as their souls entwined on the astral plane. Her's screams hurt, but Zarifah refused to let go.

You don't deserve my body, Zarifah screamed.

You're a poor disciple. I had to look elsewhere you were so weak in the end. Her's form was strong. Zarifah had to work hard against being pushed away from her own body. She wound her etheric form around the goddess as Her tried to enter the small gap between worlds and become mortal again. Her turned and Zarifah looked into the black eyes of her teacher. She saw the true plans of her beloved goddess.

Zarifah saw the Earth's soil blacken even more under the rule of Her. Earth wouldn't be restored with Her back in mortal form.

Let go, screamed Her as the gap became smaller.

Fuck you. Zarifah twisted her soul energy tighter around Her. *I can't let you return.* They struggled together. She had to do something to stop this power-hungry soul.

Then they will die. Her screamed as she saw the gap between the worlds closing, the chance for her to be mortal again slipped away.

No, they'll live. They'll find a new goddess, someone more worthy to worship. Zarifah had seen the strength in Etana.

Falling too quickly away from Earth, Zarifah felt the gap close. Her soul now free from her body, she began tumbling into the blackness, taking the goddess Her with her. Into the blackness their souls dispersed.

Overpowered by the depth of the dark and the energy of the astral plane, they were both pulled apart, separated molecule by molecule to be recycled, transformed into a new energy, one to be birthed into a new world, in a future that was being seeded.

***

Torin knelt next to Zarifah, his tears falling into her wound. Her had told him what to do. He had to follow

Her's instructions. But he now doubted what he'd done as the woman he loved lay dying. There'd been too many deaths and Her said they couldn't trust Zarifah anymore. He'd believed Her. *Her, Her, Her.* Her had tricked him. All for the sake of wanting a mortal body.

'I'm sorry.'

He couldn't feel the goddess anymore and he no longer cared. Her had been wrong. He knew that now. Zarifah had outwitted the goddess, had found the part within herself that they all had, the part that made their emotions, the part that was at the root of being human.

'Let me help.' Etana knelt down. She held a bottle of a bitter smelling liquid to Zarifah's lips, dripping the liquid into her mouth. Torin held his breath, hoping Etana could bring Zarifah back.

A tear slid down his check. 'We were all fooled by Her.' Torin looked at Zarifah. *My love, I'm sorry.* His chest constricted.

Zarifah's body suddenly arched forward and she gasped for air; her eyes fluttered open.

Torin rushed to her side. 'Zarifah you're… you're… alive?' He wasn't sure if this was a trick or not. He cradled her in his arms. 'Stay with me, please,' said Torin. 'I know the truth now.' He held her tight, willing her to stay with him. He stopped himself from praying to Her. The goddess was of no help. 'Please.'

Torin sobbed. But he didn't give up hope. It was a miracle Etana had brought Zarifah back, and he was determined to keep her here.

'Torin.' Zarifah's voice was soft.

'Stay with me.' Torin kissed her lips.

'Her was corrupted.' Zarifah's words came breathless and short.

'I know. Etana bought you back.'

Zarifah smiled weakly. 'Etana is talented.' She slipped into unconsciousness.

Torin wept.

'Don't worry, she's only sleeping,' said Etana. She rested her hand on Torin's shoulder. 'She's going to need time to heal.'

***

Zarifah leaned into Torin as he helped her to sit up in bed. *There's so much work to do.* But they wouldn't let her do anything until she had healed fully.

'Careful,' said Etana.

'Can you feel Her?' asked Torin.

'No.' Zarifah didn't miss the goodness. 'I just wish we had the teachings.' She saw the black crystal against his skin. She touched it and shivered. *It's started. They believe me.* She trembled. Torin held her closer to him. His warmth enveloped her.

'We don't need Her,' said Etana. 'We've got each other. This is a new world and we need new teachers.'

'When did you get so wise?' asked Zarifah.

'I had a good teacher.'

A tear trickled down Zarifah's cheek. 'Together we will

find a way where the soul dancers will be honoured in the future.' She rested her head on Torin's shoulder. 'Thank you for forgiving me.'

He kissed her, gently placing his lips on hers before saying, 'Only because you forgave me.'

'We should let you rest,' said Etana.

'Please stay a while longer.' Zarifah touched the cold black crystal against her skin. A reminder of how close she came to losing all that she had believed in. Zarifah gazed up into Torin's eyes. They had lost some of the shadows from being a slave. *And now I have something to look forward to.*

Acknowledgements

Thanks to my sisters for supporting my writing and taking interest in the characters I create. Thanks to my writing friends, Marianne, Maggie, Sam and Nat for listening to plot issues, reading Soul Dancer and giving feedback.

About the Author

Lilliana has poems, short stories, novellas and full length novels published around the world. She enjoys world building and creating characters for these unusual worlds.

Check out more of her work at www.lillianarose.com